# DO ME

## IRRESISTIBLE HUSBAND SERIES

## SHERYL LISTER

# ABOUT DO ME

*Staring forty in the face, Braxton Harper is accustomed to having everything in his life fall into its precise place. Only he hasn't found that special one and he refuses to settle for anything less than a woman who is his perfect match. The moment Londyn Grant dances into his life, Braxton is convinced he's found her. Kiss by sizzling kiss, the sexy doctor slowly lets her guard down. Now, if she'd only let him into her heart...*

*Londyn knows heartbreak. By day, the psychologist counsels others, but she has yet to find a way to heal her own heart. The last thing she wants is another relationship. However, sensual and sensitive Braxton tempts her to open up and, for the first time in her life, she's letting passion rule. But it's going to take a little therapeutic intervention—in and out of the bedroom—to get Londyn to see that this time she's found the real thing.*

Editor: Paulette Nunlee 5 Star Proofing
Design: Sweet 'N Spicy Designs

*For My Irresistible Husband*

# ACKNOWLEDGMENTS

My Heavenly Father, thank you for my life and for loving me better than I can love myself.

To my husband, Lance, you will always be my #1 hero!

To my children, family and friends, thank you for your continued support. I appreciate and love you!

To my author sisters, Sharon C. Cooper and Delaney Diamond. Thanks for the ride! We definitely have to do it again.

A special thank you to Dr. Praveen Prasad for sharing your expertise and time.

Thank you to all the readers who have supported and encouraged me. I couldn't do this without you.

# DEAR READER

Dear Reader ~

Have you ever wondered what if? This series started with that question and I enjoyed writing Braxton and Londyn's journey to finding love. While Braxton is ready to become that irresistible husband, London needs a little more encouragement. Think he can convince her? Hmm... I look forward to hearing your thoughts.

Love & Blessings!
*Sheryl*

sheryllister@gmail.com
www.sheryllister.com

# CHAPTER 1

"*Y*ou guys are idiots. Axel, you're too withdrawn and emotionally unavailable to women. Though you make jokes, it's probably because of how your engagement ended. Braxton, you're waiting for a *perfect* woman. She doesn't exist because no one is perfect. If you stopped being so picky, you might find someone." She stared at her brother, Colton. "And you, my dear brother, are the most self-centered man to walk the face of the earth. You guys are never getting married until you make some changes." She shook her head and walked off.

*A perfect woman?* Braxton Harper drained the rest of his beer and trained his attention on the TV mounted on the wall behind the bar showing an NBA game. From his seat at the far end of the bar near the server's station, he had a good view. After a long day, he just wanted to enjoy a Friday evening with his buddies. And he wasn't looking for a perfect woman. Hell, as of late, he hadn't been looking for *any* woman. He shot a look at his two best friends, Colton Eubanks and Axel Becker. The three men had met years ago while playing in a basketball league and had grown close since then. They usually met weekly to catch up at the Double Trouble Bar that investment banker, Colton and his sister Dani co-owned. Tonight, however, Braxton thought the name quite appropriate. Colton's sister, Dani had designated herself the resident relationship expert and was, yet again, telling them all the reasons why they hadn't found a woman to settle down with and marry. Valentine's Day had passed a week ago and tonight, she was in rare form. Once again, he tried to focus on the score rather than Dani's voice. Of course, that didn't work because she made a point of singling them out.

She'd also called Braxton picky. His mother had said the same thing. Just because he liked order and control in his life didn't make him picky. He thought of it more as being *selective*. It made sense for him to wait for the right woman rather than waste his time dating the wrong one. He could count on one hand the number of women he'd gone out with in the past six months and still have fingers left over. Not one of them had elicited an emotion other than friendship, at best. Braxton shifted in his seat. "So, she's a little more...*passionate* tonight. What happened?"

Axel lifted his glass. "Passionate is putting it mildly." The badass corporate attorney had a big heart when it came to humanitarian causes, but not so much with women after his last breakup.

"Dani is just being her usual self," Colton said, waving a hand. "Don't let her get to you. I don't."

He tried hard to dismiss her comment, but the questions nagged at him. Why couldn't he find the right woman? He was staring forty in the face and had never once experienced any of the deep emotions associated with love. In his twenties, it had been all about the sex for him, but even those encounters fell flat. When he reached his thirties, his relationships had lasted a little longer and became more about friendship and cama-raderie, but, again, something just didn't click. He had yet to meet the one woman who stimulated him on every level. Cole's voice cut into his thoughts.

"You want to shoot around tomorrow?"

"I have to attend my cousin's wedding." And he wasn't looking forward to going. At the last three family weddings, his mother had made a point of letting every woman in earshot know he was single. He expected more of the same tomorrow. If there had been any way to opt out, he would have done it in a heartbeat.

Axel chuckled. "Lots of single women attend weddings. Who knows, you might find your Mrs. Right. If you're not being too picky, that is."

Braxton grunted. "I doubt it. And I'm not picky. I'm selective. I have no problem holding out until I find the right one." He decided they needed a subject change and the three men spent the remainder of the evening discussing everything except women and marriage.

By the time he made it home, Braxton was more than a little exhausted. As a computer network architect, he'd worked overtime almost every day that week to design layouts for three clients after the other architect at the company had to take an emergency leave. Next week, he'd be meeting with doctors in a medical practice who wanted to upgrade their current system. He blew out a long breath. *It's going to be another long week.* It took him less than fifteen minutes to shower and climb into bed, but hours more to fall asleep.

Braxton felt like he'd just closed his eyes when he heard the insistent buzzing of his cell phone. Blindly reaching for it on the nightstand, he cracked one eye open and groaned when he saw his mother's name on the display. "Hey, Mom."

"Hi, baby. You're coming to the wedding today, right?"

He rolled onto his back and sighed. "Yes, Mom. My answer hasn't changed since the last three calls this week."

"It's just that your Aunt Charlene would be crushed if you weren't there."

More like his mother would be crushed because she wouldn't be able to embarrass him like she had at the last few family weddings. "And before you say it, I know it starts at two and I won't be late."

She laughed. "Well, it doesn't hurt to make sure you have the details."

A smile curved his lips. He couldn't stay irritated with her for long. "Oh, and Mom, please promise me you won't stand up in the middle of the reception and announce that I'm not married."

"Does this mean you're bringing a date?" she asked excitedly.

"No, it does not."

"Well then I don't know why—."

"Promise me, Mom," he said. When Zerlina Harper had her mind made up about something, nothing anyone said could change it.

Her heavy sigh came through the line. "Oh, alright."

"Thank you. I'll see you later."

"Bye, baby."

Braxton disconnected, tossed the phone aside, burrowed beneath the covers, and closed his eyes. It was only nine, which meant he'd gotten four whole hours of sleep. However, after dozing on and off for two hours, he gave up. He hadn't been able to get what Dani said out of his mind. Swinging his legs over the side of the bed, he sat up and tried to recall his last date. It had been before Thanksgiving—so about four months. It had been even longer since the last time he'd had sex with a woman. Strangely, he hadn't missed that as much as he did the companionship.

Deciding he'd analyzed his life enough, Braxton dressed and went to work out downstairs in the room he'd set up as a home gym. He thought about going for a run, but nixed the idea when he saw the temperatures had only risen to the forties.

Hours later, he sat in the reception hall trying to stay out of his mother's line of sight. During the ceremony, he'd seen her point him out to at least two women he knew were not family members. So far, she'd held to her promise. He checked his watch and wondered how long he had to be there. The bride and groom hadn't arrived from the photo shoot, and he still had dinner and all the formalities to get through. Rising to his feet, Braxton walked over to the bar and ordered a Jack and Coke. He turned with the glass to his lips and froze when he saw his mother heading in his direction with a woman.

"Braxton, there you are. This is Alana. I was telling her that you work with computers and she mentioned hers was having some trouble."

Alana smiled flirtatiously up at him. "It's a pleasure to meet you, Braxton. Your mother has told me so much about you and how well you're doing at your company."

"Nice to meet you." He shot his mother a quick frown.

"Maybe you can come over to my place and help me figure out what's wrong with my computer."

His mother smiled expectantly.

"Actually, I don't work directly with computers, but I'm sure if you call the tech department of your computer brand, they can better assist you. Excuse me." Braxton walked off without waiting for a response and didn't stop until he was standing outside on the balcony overlooking the hotel's garden. He gulped the drink. The woman looked pretty enough, but the moment she mentioned him "doing well," warning bells went off in his head. She couldn't have been more obvious that she had dollar signs in her eyes. After a few minutes, he went back to his table. Thankfully, the only women he encountered until they served dinner were his aunts and cousins, so he relaxed and started to enjoy himself.

His enjoyment turned out to be short-lived. As soon as dinner ended, his mother escorted two more women over. He politely discouraged any conversation. Braxton scowled at his mother as she walked away in a huff, muttering about her hard-to-please son.

A few minutes later, his older sister, Debra, passed by the table. "Mom said stop frowning, so Aunt Barbara won't think you're not having a good time."

"I'm not having a good time," he said tersely. "Mom keeps parading these women over here like we're at a Miss America contest."

Debra burst out laughing. "Sorry, baby bro. You know she just wants you to find that special woman. Then there's that whole grandchild thing. Jared and I are done, so that just leaves you. And since you'll be turning forty at the end of the month, you might want to pick up the pace." She had a fifteen-year-old daughter and a twelve-year-old son.

He scowled at her. "If she keeps pushing, I'm going to turn into a monk."

She shook her head, bent, kissed his cheek and patted it. "See you later."

Braxton leaned back in his chair. Maybe he could get his dad to talk to his mother. Something had to change. And soon. Otherwise, he was going to start boycotting all the family gatherings. They announced the garter toss and his mother's gaze trained on him. He had no intention of catching a garter or anything else and snuck out a side door until a shout went up. He poked his head in the door in time to see the groom's best man catch it. Smiling, he stepped back into the room and noticed his mother talking to another woman and pointing toward him. She'd kept her promise about not shouting it across the room, but had found another way to do the same thing. Braxton groaned. *Not again.*

"Uncle B, come dance with me."

He glanced over his shoulder and smiled at his niece, Tonya. "Absolutely. Let's show these folks how it's done." He extended his hand.

Tonya giggled. "You're the best uncle ever!" She took his hand and pulled him onto the dance floor.

He'd dance with her all evening if it helped him dodge his mother.

*Ugh! I hate weddings.* Londyn Grant moved back as far as the crowded dance floor allowed, but it still didn't create enough space between her and her dance partner. The mixture of cologne, smoke and alcohol was enough to make her nauseous. She couldn't believe she was the only one from the office here. Her coworkers—all five of them—had backed out of attending the wedding at the last minute, citing one reason or another and leaving Londyn as the only attendee at their administrative assistant's daughter's nuptials. Her sole reason for accepting the invitation had been because she had counted on having her two male colleagues to create a buffer between her and the constant flow of wannabee suitors. She had declined several of the celebrations over the past year because she'd begun feel to like prey in a nightclub, as if she wore a neon sign posted on her forehead that read, *single and lonely.* Okay, so that might have been the truth, but since her disastrous relationship ended a couple of years ago, she'd crossed men off her list. She'd take loneliness over a broken heart any day.

Another song came on and the man raised his hands in the air and did a spin move. Londyn took advantage, and while he had his back turned, snuck off the dance floor. Fanning herself, she headed to the bar for something cool. Out of her periphery she noticed a man dancing with a teen. Her steps slowed and she stood transfixed by his movements. He seemed to be enjoying himself, if the smile on his face was any indication. Tall, rich, brown skin with close-cropped dark hair, a beard riding his jaw like a shadow—giving his handsome face a dangerous edge—and a smile that would probably make the strongest sister weak. He'd discarded his suit jacket and even in the white dress shirt, she could tell he had a fabulous body. Yeah. Sexy. Londyn shook herself. *What am I doing? No men,* she reminded herself as she continued to her destination.

Minutes later, Corinne came toward her with a wide grin befitting a proud mother of the bride. "Oh, Londyn, thank you for coming." They shared a quick hug.

"It was a beautiful ceremony and they look so happy." She'd spoken with the bride and groom briefly to offer congratulations.

"Wasn't it? I'm so excited for them. My baby girl has married into a wonderful family. They're all so warm and friendly. Have you had a chance to meet some of our family?" She winked at Londyn and whispered conspiratorially, "Quite a few of these handsome devils are single from what I understand. My nephew just moved here from Florida. He's joining a law practice here. I could introduce y—"

"No," Londyn said quickly. She forced a smile. "I mean, I'll just mingle for a while, if you don't mind." She didn't do matchmaking, either. "I'll probably only stay a little longer."

"Okay, but let me know if you change your mind."

She wanted to tell the woman she didn't plan to change her mind in this century or the next, but kept the comment to herself.

"I'd better go. My sister needs something. If I don't talk to you before you leave, I'll see you on Monday." Corinne rushed off.

Thank goodness," Londyn muttered. She went back to her assigned table and sipped her ginger ale while the party continued in full swing. The DJ played a mixture of old and new school songs that had everyone either up on the floor or bobbing their heads in their seats. This was how she had envisioned her own wedding—full of love, laughter and the promise of forever. Tears burned her eyes and the old sadness bubbled up inside her, but she forced it back down. She refused to shed another tear over her ex. *The jerk.*

She continued to scan the room, smiling at a senior couple out on the dance floor grooving to Usher's "Yeah!" Eventually, everyone relinquished the floor to them and let out a series of whoops when the woman did a little shimmy.

"Go, Grandma!" a woman called out.

Everyone around the room had gotten into the action, except the man she'd seen dancing earlier. He sat a table with a heavy scowl lining his face. She wondered why. Maybe she wasn't the only one who hated weddings. Curiosity got the better of her —as a psychologist, she had an interest in human behavior—and she found herself crossing the spacious ballroom to his table.

"I thought I was the only one who hated weddings."

He glanced up at her and slowly rose to his feet. "Why would a beautiful woman like you hate weddings?"

"Probably for the same reason you do."

He lifted a brow. "Is your mother so determined to marry you off that she's bringing a string of guys around and letting them know you're single?"

"Not quite, but they've been coming anyway. May I?" Londyn asked, gesturing to the empty chair next to his. She'd spent the past two years telling herself she neither wanted or needed a man, that she had no time in her busy schedule for romance. She had devised so many excuses that she'd become adept at keeping any and every man at bay. Yet, tonight, she had purposely sought one out. A man whose mother thought he needed help. Men who looked like him didn't stay unattached long and could take his pick among women. Just from his mannerisms he seemed to be a good catch. She couldn't recall any man she'd dated standing at her approach. So why, she wondered, wasn't he seeing anyone?

"Please." He seated her then reclaimed his chair.

"Braxton." He extended his hand. "And you are?"

His large hand closed around her smaller one. *Strong and warm.* And since he seemingly wasn't interested in relationships, safe. "Londyn. Bride or groom's family?"

"Groom. He's my cousin. What about you?"

"Bride. A member of the family is my colleague."

Braxton opened his mouth, then closed it. His lips settled into a grim line.

Londyn followed his gaze and saw a woman she assumed to be his mother, a look of determination on her face, approaching with another woman. She chuckled.

He hopped to his feet. "Would you like to dance, Londyn?"

She read the plea in his eyes. "Sure. I'll help you out."

A slow grin curved his lips. "I appreciate it."

He led her out to the dance floor. Belatedly she realized the DJ had switched from the fast-paced dance songs to a slow, jazzy ballad. The moment Braxton wrapped his arms around her, she knew she'd made a mistake. He smelled good and his hard body against hers felt even better. Even in her heels, he towered over her five-foot, three-inch frame by almost a foot. He gathered her closer, keeping a respectable distance, but his thighs brushed against hers and she stifled a moan. All the emotions she'd repressed since her breakup surfaced, and for the first time in a very long while, she felt desire. Londyn was torn between wanting to flee or move closer to the man whom she now realized was anything but safe.

"So, what do you propose I do as payment?"

She looked up at him. "Payment?"

"For helping me."

Londyn averted her gaze. "Nothing, since you're helping me,

too," she said without thought. She wanted to snatch the words back as soon as they left her mouth. *Just great, Londyn. The man probably thinks you're desperate or something*, she muttered to herself. To his credit, he didn't push the issue. As soon as the song ended, she intended to thank him and leave, but he swung her out and started moving his hips to the up tempo beat of the next song. No way would she leave the dance floor now, not when it was a song by her favorite artist, Prince. The old school funk of "Musicology" made her throw her hands in the air and sing along. The DJ followed up with Michael Jackson's "P.Y.T.", Beyoncé's "Crazy In Love" and a few more classics. Londyn couldn't remember the last time she'd had so much fun. Finally, they left the dance floor.

"Can I get you something to drink?"

"Actually, I'll have to take a raincheck. I need to get going."

Braxton nodded. "How about I walk you to your car?"

"Then you can consider your bill paid in full." His deep laughter surrounded her and made her belly flip.

"I'll take that."

He placed his hand in the small of her back and guided her to the elevators and down to valet. She stole glances at him striding next to her and couldn't figure out why he needed help finding a woman. The man was fine, sexy and a true gentleman. She tried to discern how old he might be—somewhere in his mid-thirties like her she guessed based on the way he carried himself—but his unlined face didn't give anything away. Another thing she noticed about him was that he didn't talk a lot. While waiting for her car to be brought around, she asked, "How much longer are you planning to stay?"

"I'll probably be right behind you. I stayed through all the formalities, so my mom should be satisfied."

"Miss, your car," a valet said behind Londyn.

"Thank you." Londyn turned to Braxton. "Thank you for a great time, Braxton."

"Thank *you*. Maybe I can return the favor one day," Braxton murmured.

She smiled. Secure in knowing she'd never see him again, she said, "Maybe."

He helped her into the car. "Have a good evening, Londyn."

"You too." He closed the door and stepped back.

As she drove off, she glanced in the rearview mirror and saw him standing there for several seconds before turning and going back into the hotel. She couldn't believe she'd stayed at the reception for more than two hours when she had only planned to be there long enough to taste the cake and toast the newly-weds. Then again, as she noted earlier, Braxton could make a woman forget herself.

Londyn hadn't taken two steps inside her condo when her cell rang. She dug it out of her purse and smiled when she saw her friend's name on the display. "Hey, Monique. I knew either you or Felicia would be calling me tonight." She had met Monique Broussard and Felicia Holman in college and the three women had formed a bond as close as sisters.

Monique laughed. "How else am I going to get the details about the wedding? Did you meet any sexy guys?"

"I didn't go to meet any guys, sexy or otherwise, but the wedding was beautiful." She walked straight to her bedroom and kicked off her shoes. Dropping down on the side of the bed, she massaged her aching feet.

"Which is code speak for you met someone. Besides, I detected a change in your tone, so you might as well tell me, girlfriend."

"You're as bad as my mother," she mumbled. "Okay, fine. I danced with a guy the entire night. He's one of the groom's cousins."

"I *knew* it. What's his name, what does he look like and when are you two going out?"

Londyn shook her head and chuckled. "You act like this was

a date or something. We both just happened to be at the same wedding." When Monique didn't comment, Londyn sighed. "His name is Braxton, he's good-looking and seemed nice enough, and we aren't. He didn't ask for my number and I didn't give it." She told her about them dancing and him walking her to her car.

"I can't believe you, Londyn. How could you *not* give the brother your phone number, especially after he had the courtesy to walk you out?" Monique asked with exasperation.

"I'm not looking for anyone to date." She didn't plan to let another man shatter her heart.

"I know Antoine hurt you, but it's been almost two years. All men aren't like him."

"Maybe not, but I'm not ready to take that chance." She said the words even as an image of Braxton's smiling face floated through her mind. Admittedly, she'd had fun with him. Would he have turned out to be different? It didn't matter because she'd never know.

# CHAPTER 2

"Who was that woman you were dancing with last weekend at Mikel's wedding? Y'all were out on the floor for a long time."

Braxton glanced over his shoulder at Debra. "She said her name was Londyn and that's all I know." He resumed nailing a board in place. His brother-in-law, Jared, had asked him to help build a two-level deck and the two men had been at it since eight, well before the time Braxton usually left his house on a Saturday morning. Now, three hours later, they had only completed a small portion of the top level. Because of Jared's construction experience, he'd estimated that it would take about three weeks with the two of them working on weekends and Jared doing some during the week.

"Baby, if you want this deck finished sometime before spring, you need to leave Braxton alone. This weather isn't going to hold long."

Debra placed a hand on her hip. "Jared, why are you always taking Braxton's side? You're supposed to be married to me."

Jared stood and kissed his wife. "I'm not taking sides. I'm

trying to build the deck *you* wanted and you're messing with my help."

Braxton chuckled. "Right. And this help is going to want a good meal as payment." He gave her a sidelong glance. "And *not* takeout. I'm thinking fried chicken, homemade mac and cheese and some of those green beans you make with the bacon in it. Oh, and rolls. At least a half a dozen because nobody makes rolls like you," he added with a wink.

"Mmm hmm, yeah, right. You just don't want to tell me what's going on."

He threw up his hands. "Sis, there's nothing going on. We danced a few times, I walked her to her car, and that's it."

Debra studied Braxton a long moment, no doubt looking for any sign that he might be lying. Three years older, she was the only one who'd always been able to read him like an open book. "Alright. If you say so. But if you meet someone, I'd better be the first to know," she called over her shoulder as she entered the kitchen through the sliding glass door.

"Man, you two have been married for seventeen years and you still can't get your wife to stay out of other folk's business."

Jared let out a bark of laughter. "Debra stop being nosy? That'll be the day." They continued to work in silence for several minutes, then he asked, "So, is that all you really know about Londyn?"

"Yes," he answered without looking up.

"Is that all you *want* to know about her?"

Braxton wanted to say yes, but knew it would be a lie. He hadn't been able to stop thinking about her all week. From her beauty and infectious smile to her sensual voice and the way she moved her sexy body on the dance floor, she had totally captivated him. "No."

"Then just call her up and invite her out."

"I didn't get her number."

Jared whipped his head around. *"What?* You didn't ask her for her number?" He doubled over in laughter. "I can't believe it. You've been interacting with computers so long, you don't even know how to behave in the real world. Maybe you need to start spending a little less time building computer networks and actually *network."*

"I don't spend all my time with computers." Okay, so maybe over the past few months, he'd put in more hours on the job than normal, but outside of meeting up with Cole and Axel weekly and the monthly family dinners, he didn't have much else to do. After several disappointing dates, he'd pretty much stopped thinking about having a long-term relationship.

As if reading his mind, Jared asked, "If that's the case, when was the last time you were in a relationship? And I don't mean those one-and-done dates."

Braxton didn't respond.

"Like I said, you need to get out and see people. Did Londyn say who invited her to the wedding?"

"She mentioned someone in the bride's family being a coworker."

He nailed in another board. "You can always call Aunt Barbara and ask."

"I'm not that hard up for a date." Besides, he'd sensed her being tired of men trying to hit on her and hadn't wanted to fall in the same category.

Jared laughed. "If it's been that long, you just might be."

He shot his brother-in-law a dark look. "Shut up, Jared." He didn't need any reminders of how long it had been since his last sexual encounter. Fifteen years ago, he would've gone crazy without having sex at least weekly. Braxton was in the middle of a six-month drought and it hadn't bothered him as much as he'd thought. He'd be lying if he said he didn't miss the physical connection with a woman and he'd awakened more days than not hard as a rock. These days he just wanted more.

They worked for another three hours before calling it a day.

Braxton showered in one of the guest bathrooms, then sat to play a video game with his nephew, who looked exactly like his father and happened to be his namesake. The family called him JJ to avoid confusion.

"I've been practicing, Uncle B, and you're not beating me today."

"In your dreams. I was playing video games before you were born."

"Anybody can play those prehistoric games," JJ said with a grin.

Braxton eyed him. "Are you dissing my childhood games?"

He shrugged, not taking his eyes off the screen, his fingers moving nimbly over the control. "I'm just sayin'."

"Just for that, I'm going to beat you before you get to level two." He leaned forward, concentrating on blowing up every villain that had the misfortune to cross his path.

JJ scooted to the edge of the sofa and moved his body as if he were part of the game. "Ha! You missed. I'm about to pass you."

"I don't think so, buddy."

"JJ turn off that game and wash up. Dinner's ready," Debra called from the kitchen.

"*Aw, Mom!* It's not over yet and I'm about to beat Uncle B."

"You'll have to beat him later."

Braxton ruffled his nephew's curly hair. "We'll pick it up next time." He placed his controller in a basket full of remote controls and other game controllers.

Sulking, the young boy tossed his controller in the basket and stood. "Dinner is always ready at the wrong time."

He chuckled. "I happen to think dinner being ready is always at the right time. Come on, let's get cleaned up." Minutes later, they joined his sister, brother-in-law and niece at the table. "Something smells good, sis. I hope it's those biscuits I worked hard to get."

Debra rolled her eyes. "You're lucky I love you, otherwise, you'd be having fast food."

Braxton kissed her cheek. "I love you, too. You're the best big sister ever."

"I already cooked the dinner, so you can stop sucking up." Growing up, whenever Braxton wanted something, he would lavish her with compliments.

Smiling, he took a seat next to Tonya. He'd had his sister wrapped around his finger then and now. After Jared blessed the food, they filled their plates. Debra had prepared all the dishes he requested. His mother often accused her daughter of spoiling Braxton and she had been correct. Debra had been Braxton's confidante, helped him solve whatever problems he'd had and, along with their father, talked to Braxton extensively about respecting women and his responsibility in romantic relationships. He would never forget the time when she'd overheard him and a few of his high school friends laughing about one of the girls in their class. Debra had taken him aside and asked him how he would feel if those boys had said those things about her. She couldn't have made her point any clearer because he knew he would've kicked their asses. Ashamed, he'd apologized to the girl and, from that point on, had never knowingly done anything to hurt another woman. Braxton bit into a fried chicken drumstick and groaned. "This is so good."

"I know," Debra said smugly. "I may not be able to do a lot of things, but I *can* cook."

"You can do it all, baby," Jared said, grinning at his wife. "And you're the best elementary school teacher in the country."

Braxton watched the loving stares between Jared and Debra and smiled. It was the same with his parents. The older couple had been married for nearly fifty years and were still very much in love. Braxton had caught them more than once sharing a passionate kiss, and he briefly wondered if he'd find the same kind of love. Londyn's smiling face flashed in his mind. Why hadn't he asked for her phone number?

"Babe, Braxton said Londyn works with one of Lena's family members. I told him he should call Aunt Barbara and have her find out, since he forgot to get it," Jared added, not looking up from his plate.

Debra frowned. "What do you mean you forgot to get her number, Braxton?"

Braxton glared at Jared. "I didn't *forget*. I just didn't ask."

"You should've, Uncle Braxton," Tonya said. "She's pretty and, ooh, she can *dance*." She threw her hands in the air and did a move in her chair.

Four pairs of eyes focused on Braxton expectantly. "What?"

"Are you going to get her number from Aunt Barbara?" JJ asked.

"No, I'm not, so can we just enjoy dinner." He forked up some of the mac and cheese and ignored his family. But he couldn't stop the thought that crept in telling him he should put in that call to his aunt.

Friday, during lunch, Londyn stood around the table in the small office conference room with her coworkers celebrating Dr. Ralston's retirement. The man had established Ralston Mind & Wellness Center three decades ago and over the years expanded it to their current roster of five psychologists, an administrative assistant and a receptionist. They planned to wait a while before deciding whether to hire someone to replace Dr. Ralston.

"I want to thank you all for making this counseling center one of the best around," Dr. Ralston said, his voice filled with emotion. "Shawn, you were the son I never had, and I trust that under your leadership, all we've accomplished will continue."

Shawn nodded. He had been Dr. Ralston's mentee and had worked in the practice since the beginning of his career. "I'll do my best." He shifted closer to Londyn and whispered, "And I'm going to finally bring this office into the twenty-first century."

Londyn shushed him. However, she agreed the computer system needed a complete overhaul. They were still using computers Dr. Ralston had installed more than fifteen years ago.

"You know I'm right. I have a company coming in this afternoon to talk about designing a network for the office, so we can all access everything digitally and get rid of some of this paper."

She paused to clap with everyone when Dr. Ralston finished his speech, then shot Shawn a look of incredulity. "You know that's just wrong. You could've at least waited until the man left the building."

Shawn smiled and shrugged. "I scheduled it for three. Can you sit in?"

Londyn mentally went through the list of clients whose notes she needed to finish. The psychologists saw patients four days a week from eight to five, but on Fridays only until noon. The afternoons were set aside for meetings, charting and the occasional rescheduled appointments. She only had two notes to finish that afternoon. "Sure."

"I'll make sure everyone else is available, as well, and we can meet about half an hour before to discuss what we need."

"Sounds good." She moved away to join in the conversation and to give Dr. Ralston his gift. "This is for you." She handed him a small black square box with a silver bow.

"Thank you, Londyn." Dr. Ralston gave her a brief hug and untied the bow. "I'm depending on you to keep Shawn in line. He pushes a little too hard sometimes."

She chuckled and patted his shoulder. "Don't worry, I will." While Shawn exhibited a level of compassion with his patients not often seen, he tended to be less diplomatic when it came to dealing with those who threatened their wellbeing.

He opened the box and let out a hearty laugh. "Amanda will probably call to thank you herself. Pappadeaux is her favorite restaurant."

"I know." His wife had mentioned it during their annual Christmas dinner. Londyn cut a small piece of the chocolate cake Corinne had baked and stood off to the side while he unwrapped the remainder of his gifts. An hour later, Dr. Ralston packed the last of his belongings into his car and said a teary goodbye.

Londyn went back to her office, finished typing her notes, then at two-thirty, made her way back to the conference room. Shawn was already seated around the table for eight scribbling on a note pad. She sat in the chair to his right.

Shawn's head came up. "I've been crazy busy this week since I got back and forgot to ask you how the wedding went." He'd decided at the last minute to leave two days earlier for his scheduled vacation.

"It was fine, and I'm still mad that you all left me hanging."

His brows knitted together. "What are you talking about?"

"Dee, Brant, Phyllis, and Sofia all backed out. Even Dr. Ralston was a no-show. I was the only one there."

He covered her hand with his. "I'm sorry, Londyn. Why didn't you call me? You know I would've changed my itinerary for you."

She gently pulled her hand back. "That wasn't necessary."

He leaned closer to her. "Londyn, I don't know why you won't let me—"

"Please don't, Shawn. We've already had this conversation, and my answer is the same." He'd been asking her out for the past three months and she had repeatedly told her she would not date a coworker. At forty-four, his mahogany good looks still turned the heads of women whenever he walked into the room. They'd had lunch together occasionally and attended a few charity dinners, but only as friends. And she planned to keep it that way. Shawn opened his mouth to say something, but closed it when the rest of the staff filed in and claimed seats, granting Londyn a reprieve. He gave her a look that said their conversation was far from over and she returned it with one that said it was over. Forever.

"Okay, everyone, I called this meeting because someone from BroyTech Industries is coming at three to discuss getting a computer network service."

Corinne clapped her hands. "Hallelujah!" They all laughed.

"It will definitely make your job easier," Shawn said with a smile. "All of ours. We'll go around and everyone can give me their thoughts. Corinne, you can go first."

"A streamlined appointment system where I can see all the appointments at once without having to flip through five sheets of paper. Something color-coded maybe," she added thoughtfully.

Shawn continued around the table, and though Londyn knew the system they had should have been updated years ago, hearing it out loud made her realize they were doing double and triple work. Dr. Ralston was from a time when paper ruled, but they'd moved past that eons ago and it was time for the office to go digital. Her biggest concern was the security of patient records and she shared it when asked.

"Thanks, everyone," Shawn said. "Anything else?" When no one offered anything, he said, "If you think of anything else, let me know." He checked his watch. "Dee, when the representatives from BroyTech arrive, can you escort them here?"

"Sure thing." Dee had been hired as the receptionist last year when the previous one retired.

Londyn waited for everyone to leave before speaking. "Do you have any idea how much this is going to cost?"

"No, but I talked to Dr. Ralston about it yesterday and he

offered to foot the initial bill. We'd just have to pay for the maintenance. We met with Irvin right after and he said that we were in good shape financially." Irvin handled the finances.

"That was generous."

"Excuse me," Dee said.

Londyn turned and gasped softly. Standing in the doorway wearing another tailored suit and looking even more handsome than she remembered stood Braxton. Their eyes connected and a slight smile tilted the corner of his mouth. Her pulse skipped.

Shawn rose from his chair and extended his hand. "I'm Dr. Shawn Ingram."

Braxton shook Shawn's hand. "Braxton Harper."

"And this is Dr. Londyn Grant."

Londyn rose and shook Braxton's hand.

"It's nice to meet you, *Doctor* Grant."

She smiled. "Nice meeting you, as well." The slight squeeze of her hand was the only indication he gave that they'd met previously. Then again, it might have been wishful thinking on her part because she hadn't been able to get him off her mind over the past week. When he didn't return her smile or offer any other acknowledgement, she didn't know whether to be insulted or relieved. She came to the conclusion that she felt a little of both.

# CHAPTER 3

*B*raxton successfully concealed his delight in seeing Londyn again. *A psychologist.* He would have never guessed. Over the past several days, he tried to recall everything about her, but failed miserably. She was even more beautiful than he remembered. Gone was the siren in the fitted pale gray dress, with her hair flowing around her shoulders, and dance moves that aroused him in ways that continued to defy logic. Today, she wore a pair of black slacks with a long-sleeved purple sweater and her hair in a bun secured on the top of her head. Some things hadn't changed: her mocha face was just as gorgeous, her hazel eyes still sparkled and just the sight of her made his heart beat a little faster. He took it as a sign and vowed that this time he wouldn't leave without getting her phone number.

Shifting into work mode, he sat opposite her and the other psychologist. "I know your time is valuable, so let's get down to business. I'll tell you a little about our services and then you can let me know how we can help you. We specialize in designing networks tailored to your needs, whether it's starting from scratch or improving your existing system."

Braxton handed the doctors a brochure and walked them through all the details.

"We're looking at pretty much building from scratch," Shawn said. "Currently, we all have computers, but they aren't connected to each other. There are four psychologists—we have room for one more—a financial manager, administrative assistant and receptionist. Right now, when we make appointments, we have to print them for our assistant."

Braxton nodded and typed notes on his iPad. "Ideally, you'd want one system where you can all input and view the information."

"Exactly. And color-coded for each therapist to make it easier. We'd also want to store patient records digitally," Londyn said. "And network security. I want to make sure our clients' information is protected."

His gaze lingered on Londyn as she spoke. He asked several more questions and recorded the answers, his mind already thinking about the design. "What about remote access?"

Londyn chuckled. "That would be nice."

"I agree," Shawn said.

"Do you have a space to house the hardware?"

Shawn drummed his fingers on the table. "There are a couple of smaller offices that might work. Would you like to see them?"

Braxton stood. "Yes. I'd also like to see where you want to place the other computers." He followed them first to the empty rooms, the receptionist area, and finally through each office space. It wasn't until they'd stopped to talk to the administrative assistant that he made the connection that she had been the coworker Londyn mentioned, and his cousin's mother-in-law. With so many people attending the wedding and him trying to avoid his mother, Braxton never had a chance to meet the woman, so she didn't recognize him. They ended in Londyn's office. He scanned the area that held the same dark wood desk, a pair of chairs and beige loveseat as in the other offices. However, she had decorated hers with accents in varying shades of purple. A couple of plants rested on end tables and several framed certificates and degrees hung on her wall. He noticed the date on her doctorate degree and put her age somewhere in the mid-thirties.

The administrative assistant knocked on the open door. "I'm sorry to interrupt. Shawn, you have a phone call."

"Thanks, Corinne." Shawn turned toward Braxton. "Mr. Harper, I'm sure Dr. Grant can answer any questions you might have. If you'll excuse me."

"I'll most likely need to schedule another meeting to discuss the network design and get your approval before we install it."

"That's fine. Will next Friday morning at eleven work? I have something that can't be canceled in the afternoon."

Braxton opened his iPad and checked his calendar. "Yes." He added the appointment.

"Londyn?"

"I'll have to check my schedule, but I think I can be there."

Shawn nodded. "Thanks for coming, Mr. Harper. I'll see you then."

Now that Braxton had concluded his business for the day, he could shift into personal mode. He waited until both the doctor and the assistant left, then said to Londyn, "Any chance I might get you to return that favor?"

A smile blossomed on her face. "I wasn't sure you remembered me."

He wanted to tell her that he'd seen her face in his dreams at night and that she'd invaded his thoughts during the day. "I remember everything about you, Londyn. Or should I call you Dr. Grant?"

"Londyn is fine."

"Still waiting on an answer, though?"

"To what?"

Braxton chuckled. "Returning the favor."

"You're asking me to go dancing?"

He shrugged. "It doesn't have to be dancing. We could go out to dinner, see a movie, or both. Or we could do something totally different. I'd just like to take you out and get to know you."

Londyn nibbled her bottom lip, angled her head thoughtfully, but didn't answer for several seconds. "May I ask you a question first?"

"Sure."

"When you first arrived, you barely acknowledged me. Why?"

He studied her briefly, seeing a glimpse of vulnerability that hadn't been there before. The confidence she'd exuded at the wedding was one of the things that drew him and now she'd piqued his curiosity even more. "One, because my first priority in this office is business. Two, I respect your privacy. These people are your colleagues and I didn't want to assume you'd mentioned anything about us."

Finally, she said, "Okay. It's a date."

Braxton let out the breath he hadn't been aware he was holding. He didn't realize how much he wanted her to say yes. "If you'll give me your phone number, I'll call you tonight and we can discuss it. If you're available."

She rounded her desk, picked up a card and wrote on the back. "This is my cell number, and any time after seven is good."

Smiling, he accepted the card and tucked it in the breast pocket of his suitcoat. *I won't have to call Aunt Barbara after all.* His gaze dropped to the gloss-slicked lips she had a habit of nibbling on and he wanted to do the same. He took a step toward her, then stopped short, reminding himself that this was not the place nor the time. "I'll talk to you later."

"Bye, Braxton."

Pivoting on his heel, he walked out. Braxton drove back to

his office, spoke to the engineer and asked her to add his next appointment with Ralston Mind & Wellness Center. Although he would be designing the network, Gayle would be the one to install it. Afterwards, he headed to Double Trouble. Usually, the three men hung out for several hours, but tonight, Braxton didn't plan to stay long.

He finished his beer and declined a second drink.

"What's wrong with you?" Axel asked.

"Nothing. I'm cutting out early tonight."

Cole grinned. "Hot date?"

"Not exactly. I met someone and I promised to call tonight."

"Is she one of the women your mother introduced you to at the wedding?"

Braxton frowned. "No, but she was there as a guest of the bride's family." He shared the details of how they met and him not getting her phone number.

Axel swiveled on his stool to face Braxton. "How are you going to meet a woman and not get her number?"

"She gave me the impression that she was tired of men coming on to her, so I didn't want to do the same thing." He shrugged. "It worked out, though, because her office just hired us to design and install a network."

Cole swirled the contents of his glass. "What does she do?"

"Clinical psychologist."

"Brains and beauty." He lifted his glass in a mock toast.

"Exactly." Braxton stood and tossed a few bills on the bar. "I'll see you guys later."

"Good luck," Axel and Cole chorused.

"I could say the same thing to you two." He didn't need luck. He needed to know if she was that special woman he'd been searching for, the one who complemented him. He took a step and heard Cole growl under his breath. Braxton followed Cole's line of sight to where a customer stood getting a little too friendly with Malaya, one of the servers.

"Take a breath, Cole," Axel warned.

"As long as he doesn't put his hands on her, he won't have a prob... *Son of a*—" Cole leaped from the bar stool and headed to the other side of the bar.

Braxton shook his head. "Man, he's got it bad for her. I do hope that brother backs off before Cole gets to him." He could hold his own in a boxing ring due to sparring with Cole on a regular basis, but his friend had boxed semi-professionally during his college days and could handle any situation that came up. Braxton stayed in his spot a few minutes longer. Certain Cole had it all under control, Braxton said his goodbyes.

When he got home, Braxton climbed the stairs to his bedroom and changed out of his suit into a pair of sweatpants and a T-shirt. He typically only wore suits when meeting a client, opting for business casual at all other times. Starving, he loped back down to the kitchen and heated up the last of the chicken enchiladas he'd made. He typically used the weekends to plan for the week, including work, social activities, exercise and meal planning to cook enough for the week. His sister often chided him, saying he'd never find someone to share his life because he was too anal and rarely did anything spontaneously. Braxton wasn't so much anal, he just liked order as opposed to chaos.

While eating, he checked his personal email and text messages. He smiled at the photos his mother had sent from his cousin's wedding, then frowned when she wrote she hoped she'd be the next mother of the groom. He sent back a simple reply: *Very nice pictures!* Braxton finished his dinner, cleaned up and then went to his bedroom. He stretched out on his bed and dialed Londyn's number

"Hello," came the tight reply, followed by a soft moan.

He sat up straight. "Londyn, are you okay? What happened?"

"Ow, I stubbed my toe on the edge of the dresser." She

groaned.

"Do you need medical attention?"

Londyn's forced laughter came through the line. "If I did, would you come take care of me?"

Braxton lifted a brow. "In a heartbeat. Where do you live?"

"In Buckhead, near Lenox Mall."

How had they lived so close to each other and their paths never crossed? "I'm only fifteen minutes away in Druid Hill. Say the word and I'll be there."

She sighed. "I'm okay. You're so not what I expected, Braxton," she added softly.

He resumed his position and folded an arm behind his head. "Is that good or bad?"

"I'm really not sure."

"The best way to find out is for us to spend some time together. What's your pleasure?" Belatedly, he realized how suggestive the question sounded. The image of her nibbling on her lips and his reaction popped into his head. "I just meant—"

"You're fine. I know what you meant. Since I'm not sure how this toe is going to feel tomorrow, we might have to put off going dancing for another time."

Braxton smiled. Another time meant he'd have at least two dates in which to determine whether they should continue to see each other. "Then how about dinner?"

"That's sounds good. Dressy or casual?"

"This is our first date, and first dates are always dressy. Didn't you know?" She laughed, and the sound sent a strange feeling flowing through him.

"Obviously I've been hanging out with the wrong men."

"Then maybe it's time for a change." The words *with the right man* were on the tip of his tongue, but he forced them back. What was wrong with him? He typically didn't banter with women or make declarations before the first date. Or the second.

"Hmm, maybe it is. What time should I be ready?"

"How about seven-thirty?" He mentally went down the list of upscale restaurants. "Is there anything you don't eat?"

"No, and I'm partial to seafood and Mexican food."

Something they had in common. "I think I can handle that. How's the toe?"

"Still throbbing, but I'll live."

"My number is in your phone now. Text me your address and go ice your toe. Let me know if we need to postpone."

"I'm sure it'll be fine."

"I'm looking forward to seeing you again, Londyn."

"Same here," came the soft reply. "Goodnight."

"Goodnight." Braxton disconnected. A few seconds later, the cell buzzed. Londyn had sent her address. A second text came through: *Thanks for being so caring.* Smiling, he placed the phone on the nightstand. It had been a long time since he'd anticipated an evening out with a woman so much.

"How was your weekend with Derrick, Felicia?" Londyn asked, as she, Felicia and Monique sat in Monique's condo having lunch Saturday afternoon. The three friends made a practice of sharing lunch or dinner at least twice a month, as their schedules allowed.

Felicia topped a French baguette slice with ham, Colby cheese and spicy mustard. "It wasn't." She rolled her eyes and took a bite. After swallowing, she propped her elbows on the table. "Why is it that every guy I hook up with acts like someone barely out of their teens and wants to spend all his time in the club? I'm a thirty-six-year-old organizational psychologist and I work every day analyzing people to find the right fit for a company, but I can't choose a man who's the right fit for me."

Monique popped a chocolate-covered almond in her mouth.

"I hear you. Every guy I find is either intimidated by how much money I make or they think I'm going to be their sugar mama." She worked as an optometrist. "When I do find one who has potential, he always turns out to be married."

"Ain't that the truth," Londyn said, shaking her head. She had run into the same problems with the men she dated. The one time she thought she'd found the right man, it turned out to be the biggest mistake she ever made. She shuddered every time she thought about what her ex put her through. What she had allowed him to do. Londyn vowed to never put herself in that kind of position again in the name of love.

"What are you talking about, girl? Felicia, Londyn met a tall, dark and gorgeous man at that wedding she went to a couple of weeks ago. Of course, she didn't give him her number."

Felicia stared at Londyn. "Wait. What? You didn't tell me."

Londyn repeated the same thing she'd told Monique.

"I can't believe you didn't slip him your number before you hopped in the car. Any man who walks you to your car when it's not even a date deserves a little play. And since your coworker knows his family, all you have to do is ask the woman."

She studied the fruit on her plate. "I already have his number."

"*What?*" they both shouted, followed by a jumble of questions.

Londyn held her hand up. "He showed up at the office yesterday. Shawn hired his company to design and install a computer network, only I had no idea what he did until he walked in."

Monique smiled. "That had to be interesting."

"It was. At least on my part. Braxton barely acknowledged me."

"Excuse me," Felicia said with her hand on her hip. She waved a hand. "See, I can't with these men."

Londyn laughed. "Relax, sis. He explained that his first

priority was his job, and he respected my privacy in case I didn't want anyone to know." Monique and Felicia stared with their mouths hanging open.

"Oh, hell, yeah! Braxton sounds like a keeper," Felicia said, grinning.

"I don't know about that, but we're going out to dinner tonight. I was thinking something casual, since we don't really know each other, but he said the first date is always *dressy*."

Felicia peeked at her watch. "What time is he picking you up?"

"Seven-thirty, why?"

"We need to go shopping and find you a dress that'll make his eyes pop out...and a few other things. Come on, Nique. We've only got a few hours."

Monique jumped up and retrieved the charcuterie board as Londyn reached for a cracker and slice of cheese. "Hurry up and eat that." She covered it with plastic wrap and stuck it in the refrigerator. "It needs to be something that hugs her curves," she called out to Felicia.

"Hold up, y'all. I do not need to go shopping for another dress. I have some perfectly good options already in my closet." They looked at her as if she'd lost her mind and shook their heads. Felicia handed Londyn her purse and jacket, then picked up her own belongings.

Monique retrieved a jacket from the front closet and grabbed her purse. She latched onto Londyn's arm. "Let's go."

Knowing she didn't have a choice, she donned her jacket and let them lead her out. Londyn always teased her two friends about being professional shoppers. They could spend an entire day going from mall to mall without missing a beat. Londyn, on the other hand, tended to search online first to get ideas before venturing into a store. That way she would already know what she wanted. Today, however, being with her shopaholic friends paid off. It had only taken them forty-five minutes to find a black long-sleeved asymmetrical crepe dress. It fit her like a glove, left one shoulder bare, stopped just above her knees, and had a front slit that gave a glimpse of her thighs when she walked.

"Okay, you were right," she said, turning one way, then the other in the mirror.

Monique and Felicia shared a smile, and Felicia said, "I know. Now, we need shoes. This March weather is too cold for sandals, so pumps it is."

Londyn paid for the dress, then they took the escalator down to the shoe department. She searched and discarded shoe after shoe.

"I found it." Monique held up a silver rhinestone t-strap platform heel. "You need a little bling to liven up that black dress."

"How tall is Braxton?" Felicia asked.

"Around six-two or three."

"Good. Even with the four-inch heel, you'll still be a good six inches shorter."

Londyn asked an attendant for her size. She sat on one of the cushioned chairs and tried them on. They were a little higher than she typically wore and put a little pressure on her sore toe, but if they didn't do much walking around she'd be fine.

"Since we shopped in record time, we have time to get a mani-pedi."

She hooked her arm in Felicia's. "I don't know what I'd do without you guys." Their excitement had rubbed off on her and she found herself anticipating her date a little more. Her cell rang. She released her friend's arm and fished the phone out of her purse. Braxton's name flashed on the display. "Hi, Braxton." Monique and Felicia moved closer and she eased back, frowning at them. "What's up?"

"I just wanted to let you know that our dinner reservations are at seven-thirty tonight. I'll be there to pick you up at ten after seven."

She gave him instructions where to park in her building. "I'll be ready."

"So will I," Braxton said softly. "See you in a while."

As soon as she hung up, her friends squealed in excitement, causing more than a few stares. "What is wrong with you two?" she whispered.

Felicia fanned herself. "Girl, if that man looks anything like his voice, you'd better figure out a way to keep him."

"I know," Monique said. "Deep and sexy like warm honey pouring over you."

Londyn shook her head. "I can't with you guys." But she didn't deny it. Every time she heard his voice, it had her thinking about things best left alone.

Felicia laughed. "But you'd better with *him*."

"I'm going to pay for my shoes." She left them laughing.

After their visit to the day spa, Londyn picked up her car from Monique's place and drove home. She still had enough time before Braxton's scheduled arrival to make a pan of brownies for dessert—she preferred her own baking to that of most restaurants—and enjoy a soak in her Jacuzzi tub.

She applied light makeup and her favorite deep bronze lip color, then debated on whether to wear her hair up or down. In the end, she decided on the latter. Londyn slipped into the dress, then sat on the side of the bed to strap on her shoes. She winced a little when she stood. The ice she'd applied last night helped, but she still had some lingering soreness.

At exactly seven-ten, Braxton called to let her know he was in the lobby. She told him she'd meet him there, rather than have him come up. Taking a deep breath, she left and took the elevator to the first floor. Londyn spotted him immediately. The man looked better each time she saw him.

Braxton met her halfway and kissed her cheek. "You look amazing." His gaze made a slow tour down her body and back up. "*Amazing.*"

The intensity of his stare sent a flurry of sensations through her and let her know the impromptu shopping spree had been well worth it. "Thanks. So do you." And his walk—straight spine, broad shoulders and sexy with a hint of swagger. *Mercy!* He smiled. Placing his hand in the small of her back, he guided her out to where he'd parked. He unlocked the doors of the silver gray Acura sedan by remote and seated her before rounding the fender and getting in on the driver's side.

As he pulled out of the lot and onto the road, he said, "Let me know if you want me to turn the heat up. How's the toe?"

"I'm fine. And it's still a little sore, but okay."

Braxton slanted her a glance. "Glad to hear it."

The warmth inside was a direct contrast to the outside temperatures that had dipped into the low forties. They conversed softly about everything except themselves and less than fifteen minutes later, they were escorted to a booth at Chops & Lobster Bar. She placed the napkin across her lap. "This is nice. I'd always meant to come here with it being so close to home, but for some reason, it never happened."

"Well then, I hope you enjoy it." A server appeared to take their drink order. "Will you share a bottle of champagne with me?"

"Yes." Londyn waited until the server left before asking, "Are we celebrating something?"

"We're celebrating the beginning of what I hope will be a beautiful relationship."

She went still. He spoke with the assurance of a man who knew exactly what he wanted. She, on the other hand, couldn't be sure if a relationship was something she could hope for right now. However, when she recalled how he'd behaved the first time they met and how he'd reminded her that she was indeed a woman, she wanted to take the chance. "I hope so, too," she said with a smile.

# CHAPTER 4

*W*ith difficulty, Braxton dragged his gaze away from Londyn. He hadn't been able to stop staring at her in the alluring black dress that left her right shoulder bare. When she came toward him in the lobby and he got a glimpse of her toned legs and a hint of thigh from that front slit, it had been all he could do not to cancel dinner and go straight to dessert. The rhinestone heels added several inches to her height and made her legs appear longer. But he didn't miss the slight hesitation in her voice when he mentioned celebrating the beginning of their relationship and he speculated on whether it had to do with someone from her past. He picked up his menu and studied it for a few minutes. "See anything good?"

Londyn chuckled. "I see several things. Unfortunately, my stomach wouldn't be able to try them all."

He glanced up. "You're more than welcome to order a couple of things to take home for tomorrow, if you like."

"Oh, no, that's quite okay."

She observed him for a lengthy moment in what looked like puzzlement, and he thought she might say something else. Instead, she, once again, buried her head in the menu. Braxton wished he knew what she was thinking. The server returned with the champagne and filled their glasses.

"Are you ready to order, or would you like a little more time?" their waiter asked after he placed the bottle in a waiting ice bucket.

Both were ready. Londyn chose a seafood trio, consisting of lobster, salmon and crab cakes, while he opted for the bone-in ribeye with a broiled lobster tail. They both added lobster bisque for an appetizer and agreed on sharing sides of green beans and Yukon Gold mashed potatoes.

"I'll put this order in and be back with your appetizer."

"Thank you." Once they were alone, Braxton lifted his glass. "To the beginning of something beautiful and special." Londyn touched the side of his glass and lifted it to her lips. His eyes never left hers as he sipped the sparkling beverage. He couldn't explain it, but instinctively, he knew whatever he shared with her would be both of those things.

Over the meal, Londyn asked, "How long have you worked with computers?"

He finished chewing his steak and took a sip of his drink. "Since my first year in college, which would be almost twenty-two years." He chuckled at her expression that went from surprised to confusion and knew she was trying to figure out his age. I had a part-time job at an electronics store that repaired computers. But I've always been fascinated by technology."

"Are you an engineer?"

"My undergraduate degree is in computer engineering and I've worked as one in the past. I also have an MBA in information systems. Technically, I'm a computer network architect. Instead of installing the system, I'll be building it." Early in his IT career, his focus had been more on implementing and troubleshooting existing networks, but he found he enjoyed actually designing the networks and constructing roadmaps to determine what hardware and software would be used.

Londyn leaned forward. "I think that is so cool. I can't even begin to understand anything outside of *using* the computer, and even that is a problem sometimes," she added with a chuckle.

Braxton smiled. He'd heard that often. "I could say the same for your career. I'm not sure I could sit and listen to people's issues all day. How do you do it?"

"I like helping people, and I guess you can say I probably honed my skills in high school. My friends always came to me for advice, and I figured if I was going to be doling out all this good counsel, I might as well get paid for it."

He laughed. "Good point. I can tell you're very good at what you do." During the meeting, while the other doctor had been focused on the system, itself, her concern had been for the safety of her patients' information.

"I hope so."

There it was again, that hint of sadness he'd noticed before. He didn't want to ruin the evening, so he refrained from asking about it. Besides, they didn't know each other well enough for her to confide in him. The conversation tapered off as they finished eating.

Londyn dabbed the napkin to the corners of her mouth. "That was so good. Thank you."

"You're welcome. Would you like anything else?"

"No, thank you. I need to leave room for the dessert I made for us."

He lifted a brow. "You made dessert?"

"Yes," she said, her brown and green flecked eyes shimmering. "I guess I should've asked what you like first, but I made brownies."

A smile made its way across his face. "Brownies are one of my favorite desserts. Along with peach cobbler, apple pie, pound cake, chocolate chip cookies..." He waved a hand. "You get the picture."

Leaning back against the booth, she laughed. "Yeah, I get it. You like dessert." She propped her elbows on the table, braced her chin on her hands and whispered conspiratorially, "I'll let you in on a little secret." She made a show of looking around. "So do I. They're my weakness, especially brownies topped with ice cream and a swirl of chocolate syrup." Londyn placed her hand over her heart and pretended to swoon.

Laughter poured out of Braxton. He liked this woman. "Far be it from me to keep a woman from her prized dessert." He signaled a waiter, paid the bill and drove back to her place.

He realized two things when he entered her condo: her office style matched her home, and she liked purple. The varying shades of the color had been incorporated into the furnishings and accents, and provided a warm, homey feeling. "I like your home. How many bedrooms?" The living room and den area were connected by a partial wall that held an electric fireplace. Another smaller room behind the den had been set up as an office space.

"Thanks. Just one. Less to clean. But I love living on the top floor because of the privacy and I don't have to worry about my neighbors stomping above my head." Londyn hung her coat in the closet, reached for his and did the same. "Have a seat, and I'll bring the brownies out."

"How about I help you?" Once again, she gave him a strange look. "Is there something wrong? That's the second time you've given me that look." An embarrassed expression crossed her face. She disappeared around a corner and into the kitchen. Braxton shoved his hands in his pockets and followed. "If I've done anything to make you uncomfortable, I apologize."

She paused in removing the clear plastic wrap from the glass dish holding the brownies. "You haven't done anything. I guess you caught me off guard with your offer. Not many men would, and especially on a first date. Just like when you invited me to buy an extra entrée if I wanted when that bill was already going to be expensive." She shrugged. "You're different."

*What kind of men has she been dating?* "I'm just who I am, Londyn." Braxton closed the distance between them and tilted her chin. "If I date a woman, she can expect to be treated special." He felt the slight tremor in her body and fought the overwhelming desire to wrap his arms around her. Stepping back, he pointed to the dish. "I can say the same about you. I've never had a woman bake dessert on a first date. Actually, it's never happened and I can't tell you how much I appreciate it." For a few charged seconds, neither of them moved.

Londyn cleared her throat and set out bowls and spoons. "Don't thank me until you taste them. You have two choices for ice cream—vanilla or cookies and cream."

"I'll take the cookies and cream. Might as well get my full chocolate fix."

"A man after my own heart," she said, taking the container out of the freezer.

If things worked out as he hoped, she just might be that woman. While she cut and placed a warmed brownie in each bowl, he dished the ice cream, then drizzled the chocolate syrup on top.

She grabbed the bottle and added enough to cover her ice cream completely. "Don't be stingy."

Laughing, he carried the bowls to the dining room table while she returned everything to its place. Braxton removed his tie and stuck it in his pocket, then unbuttoned the first two buttons on his shirt. He seated her first, then took his own. "Okay. The test." He dug below the mounds of ice cream and scooped up the brownie. The rich, moist treat tasted so good he groaned. "A plus, Dr. Grant."

"Why thank you, Mr. Harper."

Smiling, they enjoyed the decadent dessert while laughing

about their favorite foods to cook. While she preferred baking, he enjoyed preparing main courses.

"I can bake anything from breads and cakes to pies and everything in between. But ask me to cook chicken, and you're going to get it either baked or fried. The end. My steaks end up being either under or overcooked. The only thing I can do reasonably well is seafood. Wait, let me rephrase that...I can do shrimp and bake or broil salmon."

She had him at the mention of bread. In his mind, there was nothing like freshly baked bread in any form. He propped his forearm on the table. "I have a proposal for you."

"What kind of a proposal?" She licked chocolate off the spoon.

Braxton's body reacted with lightning speed. What made it even more arousing was that the act had been done innocently. For a moment, he lost his train of thought. "How about for our next date, I cook dinner and you make dessert? We can do it at my place."

A smile blossomed on her beautiful face and she pointed her spoon his way. "You've got yourself a deal. Just let me know when."

"Next Saturday. That'll give us time without having to rush. If you text me the list of ingredients for whatever dessert you're going to make, I'll pick them up when I go to the grocery store."

"You're going to allow me to cook in your kitchen?"

"Sure, why not? Or is this another one of those things guys don't do again?"

"I'm afraid so," she answered with a chuckle. "House or condo?"

"Townhouse."

"How many bedrooms?"

"A couple more than yours." Braxton didn't think she'd react the same, but every time he told a woman that he lived in a two-story home with four bedrooms, four baths, and over three thousand square feet of space, she started planning how fast she could move in, saying, "that's too much space for just one person." He'd rather Londyn see it for herself. "Is it a date?"

"Yes, but I'll pick up the ingredients myself because I don't know what I'm going to make yet."

"Okay. We can make a day of it. I'll pick you up at three."

"Works for me."

He polished off the remainder of his dessert, and they talked for another two hours. It was nearly midnight when he reluctantly stood. Braxton wanted to talk to her all night. He loved the sound of her voice. It was soft, comforting and perfect for the career she'd chosen. "I should get going." He picked up their bowls and carried them into the kitchen.

"Just place them in the sink. I'll rinse them and put them in the dishwasher later."

She leaned against the wall in the sexiest pose he'd seen in quite some time: arms folded, one leg crossed, exposing a firm thigh, and head tilted to one side with her hair partially covering her face. Braxton took her hand and walked toward the front. She handed him his suitcoat and he slipped his arms into the sleeves. "Thank you for your company this evening, Londyn. I really enjoyed myself."

Londyn placed a hand on his arm. "Thank *you*, and I did, too. I'm looking forward to next week."

He had told himself he would go slow, just a kiss on the cheek and leave, but when he saw her doing that lip nibbling thing he lost all reason. He wanted to taste her lips, soothe that spot himself. Sliding his arm around her waist, he drew her closer. "May I kiss you goodnight?"

"Yes," she whispered at the same time his head descended.

Braxton was supposed to kiss her, not devour her like he'd done the brownie sundae, but he couldn't help it. As soon as their lips connected, he was lost. His tongue stroked hers and delved deeper to claim every area of her mouth. The lingering sweetness from their dessert only heightened the pleasure. He eased back, gifting her with butterfly kisses along her jaw, then lifted his head. "Sleep well." *At least one of us will*, he told himself as he made his way to his car.

～

Friday morning, Braxton arrived at the wellness center with the engineer, Gayle Ross, ten minutes before their scheduled appointment. While waiting, Gayle showed him the latest pictures of her six-year-old daughter.

"I can't believe how much she's grown. The last time I saw her, she was still in diapers."

Gayle laughed. "Those days are long gone, thank goodness."

Their conversation ended when Shawn and Londyn entered. He'd never had a problem keeping his professional face on, but today it was all he could do not to haul Londyn into his arms and kiss her like he'd been fantasizing since he'd walked out of her condo a week ago. He rose to his feet to greet them. "Dr. Ingram and Dr. Grant, I'd like to introduce you to Gayle Ross. She'll be the engineer installing your network." A round of greetings ensued. "Let's get started." Braxton detailed his design, answered questions and made changes based on their responses. Gayle then shared her timeline for the installation, estimating a week to ensure the system was working properly. Braxton finished by saying, "We'll schedule monthly maintenance, but will be available for any concerns or problems."

"Sounds good," Shawn said. "Ms. Ross, would you be able to work out a schedule with each of the staff, so we can have minimal interruptions in seeing our patients? You can speak with our assistant."

"Of course. If she's not busy, we can talk as soon as we're done here."

"Thank you." Braxton fixed his gaze on Londyn. "Do you have anything you want to add?"

"I think we've covered everything."

He noticed Londyn did her best not to look his way when she answered. The one time he caught her staring during the meeting, she turned away quickly. He smiled inwardly.

Shawn stood and everyone followed suit. He shook Braxton's hand and gestured for Gayle to follow him.

Their departure left Braxton and Londyn alone. She seemed nervous, unsure. "What time is your lunch?"

"I usually go around noon. My next patient is at one."

"May I treat you to lunch? I saw a deli within walking distance."

"I'd like that. Let me get my purse, and I'll meet you out front."

He watched the sway of her hips in the gray slacks as she passed and smiled. He followed her out and stopped to let Gayle know he was leaving.

"I'm ready."

Braxton spun around at the sound of Londyn's voice. She had donned a jacket to ward off the cool temperatures. He held the door open for her and they started up the block. He entwined their hands. "Are you okay?"

Londyn smiled a little. "Yeah. It's crazy, but I feel like a teen sneaking out with the boy I like, instead of a thirty-six-year-old woman." She shook her head.

"If it makes you feel better, today was the first time I've ever wanted to kiss a woman while I was supposed to be working." They shared a look and burst out laughing, easing the tension. "You look much younger than thirty-six."

"That comment will get you your own pan of brownies."

He kissed the back of her hand. "If I said you look a decade younger, would that get me two pans?"

She rolled her eyes and smiled. "No, because I know I don't look *that* young. Since we're talking ages, how old are you?"

"Almost forty."

She squinted her eyes.

"What are you doing?"

"I don't see any gray hairs, so you can't be that old," she said, trying to suppress a giggle.

Braxton stopped walking. "Are you calling me *old?*"

"No way. And if I were, I'd say it *after* my belly was full."

Laughing, he hugged her and dropped a kiss on her hair. "Come on." They found the shop fairly crowded. "Why don't you find us a table while I order."

"Okay." Londyn told him what she wanted, then hurried over to snag a table that had been just vacated.

A few minutes later, he placed the tray holding their meal on the table and slid into the chair across from her. They ate in silence for a while, then he decided to ask the question that had been bugging him since he saw a brochure listing her specialties. "I see you provide treatment in a variety of areas and I was curious about something. How did you decide on pornography addiction, and when did that become a diagnosis?" During his college years, he'd watched it, but never thought of it as an issue.

"It's not recognized as an official diagnosis by the American Psychiatric Association, but the research suggests that behavioral addictions are serious and pornography is no exception. Just because someone indulges in watching it every now and then doesn't make it an issue. It's when the amount of time that person spends watching it keeps growing and they're on pornography sites for hours on end, and he or she starts neglecting their other responsibilities." She picked up a stray piece of tomato and ate it. "It can start from something as simple as being bored or because they're depressed, lonely."

Braxton frowned. "I never thought of it that way."

"Most people don't. Home life is affected, as well, especially when the person insists that the romantic or sexual partner view the porn and or acts out the fantasies even though that person may not want to do so. Or when it gets to the point where the person needs to view porn in order to enjoy sex."

He froze. His brain went into overdrive. He thought back to the years that he'd indulged. It started with a couple of his buddies renting the movies on weekends as a way to unwind, then for about four years, Braxton had watched them on his own when he had nothing to do. At the time, his relationships hadn't lasted past the three-month mark. And the sex... It had never been fulfilling. His heart started pounding. Was his lack of fulfilment somehow tied to a subconscious fantasy he'd expected the women he'd had sex with to live up to and when they didn't, he walked away? Even when he had stopped watching it and thinking about it, he couldn't put his finger on why his liaisons were short-lived. A sense of sadness and shame washed over him. He prided himself on treating women with respect and he would never knowingly hurt a woman in that way. Even though he had never asked any of them to "perform" any acts, or brought the subject up, parts of him wanted to find those women and apologize. Braxton pushed his sandwich aside, his appetite now gone. A touch on his hand drew him out of his musings.

"Are you okay? I'm sorry if I'm boring you. I tend to get a little passionate on the subject," Londyn said with a rueful smile.

"I'm fine. Just thinking about what you're saying, and you should be passionate about your work. You never did say why you chose to specialize in this area."

She hesitated briefly. "Someone I knew was in a relationship with a man who had a pornography addiction. He forced her to watch it, then wanted her to reenact the scene and berated her for not *performing* it right. I wanted to help her."

Braxton reached for her hand. "And did you?"

"I'm working on it." She gave his hand a squeeze. "I'd better get back." She pointed at his half-eaten sandwich. "You barely ate."

He waved her off. "I'll finish it later." He took it to the counter and had the sandwich wrapped to go. On the way back, he was still thinking about his startling revelation. Not wanting to dwell on it, he asked, "Have you decided what dessert you're making tomorrow?"

Londyn gave him a bright smile. "Yep, but I'm not telling." She leaned into him. "But it's going to be *sooo* good!"

Every time she opened up this way, it drew him to her a little more. "You are such a tease," he said with a chuckle.

"And I can back it up, too." As if she realized what she'd said, she clapped a hand over her mouth. "That is not what I meant. I was talking about cooking."

Still laughing softly, he said, "I'm talking about *cooking*, too."

Londyn stared at him a long moment. "I'm not even going to touch that."

He held the office building door open for her to enter first. "Neither am I. At least not yet." She whipped her head around and their eyes connected. They both knew the conversation had shifted from physical food to another kind of hunger. Braxton took a step, intending to kiss Londyn goodbye, then remembered they were standing in the lobby with the receptionist's eyes glued to them and moved back.

As if reading his mind, she said, "Ah, I think we should save that for another time."

"I agree. " And he planned to make up for it.

# CHAPTER 5

*W*hile Londyn prepared for her next client, a riot of emotions assailed her, one surprising and the other, unwelcomed. Teasing with Braxton had her body in an uproar. For so long, she'd told herself that passion had no place in her life, but there was something about him that made her feel safe exploring her sexuality again. She had wanted nothing more than to have him kiss her like he'd done after their date and for the first time in her life, she hadn't cared that they were standing in the middle of her workplace. Public displays of affection had never been her style, but she would have gladly broken her rule to feel his lips on hers. The second sentiment evoked the same pain and bitterness as it had almost two years ago. She had meant only to clinically answer Braxton's questions, but somehow her own feelings had worked their way into the conversation.

She closed her eyes and drew in a couple of deep breaths, then let them out slowly, gradually regaining her composure. A minute later, she was back in control. Londyn pulled the file for her next patient. This would be the first session for a couple who listed marital problems as their reason for seeking out counseling.

Londyn's intercom buzzed. She hit the button. "Yes."

"Dr. Grant, Mr. and Mrs. Stephens are here for their one o'clock appointment."

"Thank you, Dee. I'll be right out." She straightened her desk and walked out front where two couples waited. "Mr. and Mrs. Stephens?" An African American couple who looked to be around Londyn's age stood. Smiling, she shook their hands. "Hello, I'm Dr. Grant. Please follow me." She escorted them to her office and closed the door. "Please have a seat." She rounded the desk and gestured to the two chairs across from her. Londyn observed them. The man's body language and heavy scowl told her he didn't want to be there, while his wife bore an expression of worry. "Why don't you tell me a little bit about why you're here."

The man shot a glare at his wife. "*She* wanted to come. I'm fine."

"Mrs. Stephens?" Londyn prompted.

"We're having intimacy problems," the woman whispered. She paused, her lips trembling. "He watches those movies, then wants me to, to..." She trailed off. "I'm not a porn star and I don't want to be one. I just want to have normal sex." Mrs. Stephens swiped at a tear running down her cheek.

"Mr. Stephens, would you—"

He shot up off the chair. "You saying I'm not normal?" he shouted. "Just because you're too prim and proper to get your freak on doesn't make me the bad guy. I'm trying to help you," he added with a look of disgust.

"Mr. Stephens," Londyn started, keeping her voice calm and even, "I'm going to ask you to please lower your voice and have a seat."

Mr. Stephens stared at Londyn, then threw up his hands. "I'm out. I don't have time for this bullshit." He stormed out.

His wife burst into tears and Londyn handed her the box of tissues she always kept handy. It took a few minutes for the tears to slow then stop.

"What am I going to do, Dr. Grant?"

"I can't tell you what to do, Mrs. Stephens. That will have to be your decision. How long have you two been married?"

"Three years."

"How long has his watching pornography been an issue?"

She twisted the tissue in her hands, shredding it in the process, but kept her head lowered. "He was watching when I met him, but only sometimes, I think. Then, when we got engaged, I wanted us to stop having sex for the two months before our wedding. He got mad, and then I found out he was going online all the time, even on our dates." She met Londyn's gaze. "I figured once we got married, he'd stop because we'd be having sex again."

Londyn wanted to tell the woman that she should have paid attention to the red flags her husband had clearly been giving her. "Did it stop?"

She shook her head.

"Mrs. Stephens, what would you like to see happen in your marriage?"

"I want my husband to change." She scooted back in the chair and stood. "I have to go. I don't want him to leave me."

Londyn followed suit. "You still have twenty minutes left in your session."

Mrs. Stephens divided her gaze between the chair and the door. The latter won out when the woman rushed out with a hushed, "I'm sorry."

*I want my husband to change.* Mrs. Stephens' plea for her husband to change wasn't going to happen unless the man first acknowledged he had a problem. She closed her eyes. She knew that truth better than anyone. Straightening, she typed a short note of the session and prepared for the next one.

Thankfully, the remainder of her sessions had been uneventful. Londyn stretched to relieve the kinks in her neck and back. As soon as she finished one last chart, her workweek would be over. A knock sounded on her partially closed door. "Come in." She smiled when Shawn walked in. "I thought you were leaving early today."

Shawn propped a hip against the edge of her desk and folded his arms. "I was, until I heard all the commotion coming from your office earlier. I wanted to make sure you were okay."

"Just someone not wanting to be here. You know the drill."

"Unfortunately, I do." He glanced down at his loafers, then back up at her. "What are you doing this evening?"

"Grocery shopping, then relaxing." The conversation with Braxton, followed by the Stephens had opened up old wounds and she needed some down time.

Edging closer, his voice dropped to a lower register. "How about dinner? Just the two of us."

"I don't think that's a good idea." Again, she had no intention of letting him believe there could be anything between them except friendship.

"Your answer wouldn't happen to have anything to do with Braxton Harper, would it?"

"No, and why would you think that? I've told you more than once that we would only be friends."

"And if we didn't work together?"

Londyn scanned Shawn's handsome face and found herself comparing him to Braxton. While her colleague was outspoken and a little arrogant and didn't elicit anything other than a fondness reserved for a friend, the man she planned to share an afternoon with could make her pulse skip with merely a smile. Braxton exuded a quiet strength that drew her in ways she couldn't explain. Realizing Shawn was still waiting for an answer, she said, "My answer would be the same."

"I saw you two holding hands this afternoon coming from the deli."

She cut him a look. "What? Were you spying on me or something?"

Shawn let out a long breath. "No, Londyn. I just happened to be leaving the office. I have to say I'm a little disappointed because I think that we'd make a perfect couple. He works pretty fast. I've been asking you out for months and he waltzes in here once and you go out with him just like that." He snapped his fingers.

Londyn laughed. "Not that it's any of your business, but I met Braxton before he *waltzed* in here." She held a hand up when he opened his mouth to speak. "This conversation is over. Get out of my business, Shawn. I don't ask you about the women you date, and I expect the same courtesy."

He grinned sheepishly. "Point taken. Be careful, Londyn. I don't want to see you hurt."

She didn't either, which is why she planned to take things slow with Braxton. Their earlier conversation came back to her. *Neither do I. At least not yet.* Without saying so directly, he let her know that he felt the chemistry between them as strongly as she did. His words teased her and tempted her to not only *touch*, but to also taste, feel...

"Londyn."

Shawn's voice snatched her out of her lustful thoughts and heat filled her face. "Sorry. Just thinking about how much more I need to do here before leaving," she lied.

He straightened. "I won't hold you. Have a good weekend."

"You, too."

Hands in his pockets, he left with a wistful smile, closing the door softly behind him.

Londyn finished charting, locked the files in her desk and headed out. She shopped in record time and made it home by seven. After consuming the grilled chicken Caesar salad she'd picked up at the grocery store, she cued up her favorite playlist and started the prep work for tomorrow's desserts. She planned to make the dough needed for a peach cobbler tonight, refrigerate it overnight and assemble everything once she got to Braxton's place. She had a couple of other surprises, too.

She danced and hummed under her breath as Jilly from Philly—the nickname bestowed upon powerhouse singer Jill Scott—belted out "Shame." Londyn mixed the ingredients in between shaking her hips. She and Jill were jamming so tough it took Londyn a moment to hear the ringing on her iPad indicating a FaceTime call. She paused the music and smiled when she saw her mother's name.

"Hey, Mom. How are you and Dad enjoying the Bahamas?" They were ten days in to a month-long stay in the country.

"Hello, my darling daughter. Oh, my goodness, we're having a fabulous time. If I had known how nice it would be to sleep in, then get up just to lounge on the beach and eat copious amounts of food, I would've retired years ago."

She laughed. "Well, you look great." Last summer, Drs. Dwight and Paulette Grant had sold the general practice they'd established twenty-five years ago to enjoy the fruits of their labor while they were still in reasonably good health.

"Hey, baby girl." Her dad poked his head in the screen.

"Hi, Dad."

"You doing okay?"

"I'm fine. Just jealous I can't be there enjoying all that warm weather," Londyn said with a mock pout.

"Keep living," her mother said. "You'll get there. Have we missed anything?"

She hesitated for about two seconds before blurting, "I met someone." She hadn't planned to say anything yet. For all she knew, whatever they had going could be over long before her parents returned and she didn't want to have to explain another failed relationship.

Paulette's gaze softened. "Oh, sweetheart. That's good news…isn't it?" She searched Londyn's face looking for whatever mothers did when concerned about her child. Though Londyn never fully disclosed what happened with her ex, her mother knew that Londyn had been hurt badly enough to call off the wedding three months before she and Antoine were scheduled to exchange vows. Fortunately, the invitations hadn't gone out and saved her from further embarrassment.

"Yes. His name is Braxton Harper and, so far, he seems very nice. I met him at the wedding."

"When I asked you about the wedding, you never mentioned meeting someone."

She kneaded the dough as she talked. "That's because we only shared a couple of dances and didn't exchange phone numbers. We met again when the company he works for was hired to design a computer network for the office."

"It's about time," she muttered. "I don't know why Harold continued to operate that office the same way we did three decades ago. I'm sorry baby. Go ahead and tell me about this young man."

Londyn chuckled. She flattened the dough and wrapped it in plastic wrap. "We've only gone out twice, so we're still getting to know each other."

"Is that dough I see?"

"Braxton and I are having dinner tomorrow. He's going to prepare the meal and I'm making a peach cobbler for dessert."

"Hmm, I see. Where is this dinner taking place and how old is Braxton?"

"His place, and he said almost forty, so either he's thirty-nine or close to it. What did you mean by 'I see'?" Her mother had a strange expression on her face.

"I'm looking forward to meeting him when we come home."

"That's almost a month away. I don't even know if we'll still be seeing each other by then."

"You will," she said emphatically. "And, as I said, your father and I will be looking forward to meeting him. I have to run, sweetheart. Your father and I are going downstairs to the lobby to have drinks and listen to music. The resort has a band playing tonight."

Londyn shook her head. "When I grow up, I want to be like you and Dad. Love you guys."

"Love you more. Talk to you soon."

Before the connection ended, she heard her father say something. Whatever it was had her mother giggling like a schoolgirl. After more than four decades of marriage, her parents still sometimes acted like newlyweds. A pang of sadness hit her. She wanted that same kind of love.

Braxton woke up Saturday morning with more energy than he'd had in months. Instead of going over to his sister and brother-in-law's house, he had told Jared he'd be there to help finish the deck tomorrow, leaving him free to make sure everything was perfect for his date with Londyn. The person who cleaned his home twice a month had come and gone, saving him from having to do the task himself. After she left, he'd jumped into his car and didn't stop to analyze why he was driving twenty miles to a meat market for prime grade ribeye steaks because Londyn had mentioned not being able to cook them well. He seasoned the meat and placed the plate in the refrigerator next to the ones holding the cracked lobster and vegetable kabobs. The temperatures were slated to reach the sixties, so he'd planned to prepare the entire meal on the grill. He would've preferred to eat on the patio, as well, but it would be too cool by evening.

He still hadn't been able to convince her to tell him what she intended to make for dessert and his mouth watered, hoping it would be more of those delectable brownies. Even if she'd made something else, he didn't doubt it would be just as good. Braxton cleaned up the kitchen and drove to the gym where he, Cole and Axel met to shoot around on the basketball court.

Both his friends were already on the court when Braxton arrived. After a round of greetings, the three men practiced shooting free throws, and three-pointers.

"How are things going with…what's her name again?" Cole asked as he sank a corner shot.

Braxton retrieved the ball and hit a shot from the opposite corner. "Her name is Londyn and they're going well. We're having dinner at my place tonight."

Axel snatched the ball down from the rim after Cole's missed shot. "First, I thought you said last night that you were picking her up at three. Isn't that a little early for dinner? And second, you're taking a woman to your house. Are you good with that?"

"We're cooking first, and, yes."

"Bro, you remember what happened the last time you took a woman to your house," Cole said, shaking his head.

He remembered with exceptional clarity. He and Taryn had been dating for close to three months when he made the mistake of inviting her over for dinner and a movie. He should have known the woman was all about his material wealth and how she could tap into it by all the questions she kept asking about where he lived. The moment she stepped across the threshold, she started talking about parties, engagements, and babies. She'd told him he had the perfect place for a family and that, with her being thirty-two, she wanted to have at least two children, so they needed to get started. The only thing he started was the engine in his car when he took her home. That had happened three years ago and, since then, other than family, no other woman had entered his private space. "Londyn is nothing like Taryn."

Axel shot him a look of disbelief. "How do you know? You just met the woman."

"I just know. Is that the approach you're taking with Naphressa?"

"Our situation is different." He tossed the ball to Braxton.

"All I know is she makes me feel something more than I ever have and I like being with her. Cole, what about you and Malaya?"

"I'd love to invite her over, but…" Cole let the sentence hang. Both Braxton and Axel knew how Cole felt about Malaya. "It's pretty interesting that we're all starting new relationships."

"And when Dani finds out, she's going to take credit," Braxton cracked.

"No doubt."

The three men laughed, finished the game and parted ways in the parking lot.

Braxton went home, showered, then left to pick up Londyn. This time, he went up to her unit.

"Hi. Come on in," Londyn said after opening the door. "You have to be the most punctual person I've ever met. Are you ever late to anything?"

He brushed a kiss over her lips and smiled. "I try not to be late, if I can help it."

"I need help carrying everything."

He stopped short upon seeing two large totes and a cooler filled with ice. "Exactly what are you making that requires all of this? You didn't need to go through all this trouble for a dessert. More of those brownies would've been enough."

"You'll see. Let's go. I'm anxious to get this party started."

Her comment caused Braxton, for a brief moment, to wonder whether it might indeed be too soon for an invite, but he dismissed the notion as quickly as it entered his mind. He helped her into her jacket, then picked up the cooler and one of the totes.

"I've been waiting all week to find out what we're having for dinner." She grabbed the remaining tote and slung her purse over her shoulder. Facing him, she said, "I just want you to know how much I like spending time with you."

She came up on tiptoe and kissed him and he lost a piece of his heart.

# CHAPTER 6

"When you said you had a couple more bedrooms than mine, I was expecting a…a bachelor pad of some sorts, not all this." Londyn waved her hand around as they stood in the hallway on the second floor. His two-story townhouse had been elegantly decorated in varying shades of gray with black accents. Even though it had a masculine look, it still had a warm, homey feel. The four-bedroom, four-bath home had spacious living and family rooms, master bedroom with sitting area, home gym and a mudroom entrance with plenty of shelving and shoe cubbies. Each of the secondary bedrooms had en-suite bathrooms. "It's beautiful and amazing." She had wondered how, at almost forty, had he kept in such good shape. The fully equipped home gym had answered her question.

"Thanks."

Braxton took her hand and led her back downstairs to the state-of-the-art kitchen. She wandered over to the window. The back deck and private yard would be the perfect place to unwind when the weather warmed. She could fit three of her thousand square-foot condos in the house and still have square footage left over. It seemed too big for one person. "Have you ever been married?"

Braxton glanced around the open refrigerator. "No."

"Kids?"

"No," he said with a laugh. "If I had any children, I would've told you about them upfront." He placed several plates on one of three long counters. "What makes you think I've been married or have kids?"

"This place has enough space for a family of six without being crowded."

"My niece and nephew spend some weekends here, which is why two of the bedrooms are decorated."

She thought back to him dancing with the teen. "Was your niece the one you were dancing with at the wedding?"

"Yes. Tonya is fifteen going on twenty-five. My nephew, Jared is twelve. I try to give my sister and brother-in-law a break so they can have some time away occasionally."

"That's sweet. Do you have any other siblings?" Londyn moved over to the other counter when he'd placed her bags and started unloading.

"Just Debra. She's three years older and, when she's not acting as if she's my second mother, she's pretty cool."

Propping her hip against the counter, she smiled. "At least you had a companion. Try being the only child of two doctors."

"Now I don't have to wonder where you get your brilliance." Braxton leaned over and peered inside the cooler she had just unzipped.

"They are definitely brilliant. They sold their practice last year and are currently spending a month in the Bahamas. What do your parents do?"

"Both are retired—dad from engineering and mom, education. So are you going to finally tell me what we're having?"

Grinning up at him, she said, "I guess I can tell you what I'm making." She pointed to each one as she spoke. "There's dough for both a peach cobbler and a loaf of French bread, sweetened peaches and the mixture for homemade vanilla ice cream."

His eyes lit up. "Homemade ice cream? I don't have an ice cream machine."

Londyn winked at him and held it up. "Not to worry. I brought my own." She placed it on the counter and lowered the cylinder containing the mix inside. She gently squeezed his biceps. "Yep, good muscles. You're going to need them to crank the machine."

Throwing back his head, Braxton roared with laughter. "You are something else."

The sound of his deep laughter made her belly quiver. "And so are you." Slowly, his laughter faded. He stared down at her, not bothering to hide the passion in his eyes. She tilted her chin and wasn't disappointed when he covered her mouth in a sweet, gentle kiss that stirred not only her body, but her heart. She wound her arms around his neck as he pulled her closer. His hand caressed her spine, moved down to her hips, then found its way around front to her center. The thin cotton crop pants she wore were no match for his skillful fingers as they slid back and forth over her core, creating a pulsing that increased by the second. Londyn moaned and widened her stance as liquid fire spread through her. He deepened the kiss as his fingers sped up their movements. An orgasm hit her without warning and her knees buckled. She cried out as spasms shot through her body. Only his tightened grip kept her from sliding to the floor. At length, he lifted his head, but didn't release her. Londyn's body continued to tremble and her breathing came in short gasps. *Incredible!* If he could make her come just from touching her on the outside of her clothes, she didn't want to think about what would happen if they were both naked.

"Now, that's my kind of cooking," Braxton murmured. "But I think we'd better focus on the real cooking before we get into any more trouble."

She opened her mouth to tell him if he could promise more of this kind of trouble, she was all for it, but he placed a finger on her lips.

"It's not time yet, baby. I don't want either of us to have any regrets," he said, cradling her face in his palms.

"I won't regret being with you, Braxton." She wouldn't she realized, but she continued to harbor lingering fears and she didn't want them to interfere with their developing relationship.

He ran his thumb over her bottom lip. "Can you tell me with certainty that you're ready for us to take this to the next level?"

Londyn sighed. As much as she wanted to say yes—because it had been a long two years since she'd shared her body with any man—she knew in her heart she wasn't quite ready. "No."

Braxton smiled and pressed a lingering kiss to her forehead. "I didn't think so. We've got time and when it's right we'll both be ready."

Where had this man been all her life? Most others would have had her in their beds and naked—particularly since she could feel his throbbing erection pressed against her—but Braxton appeared to be from a throwback era of men who took time to court a woman. Maybe that's why it had been so easy for her to let her guard down. In that moment, Londyn fell a little harder. "Thank you." She backed out of his embrace.

"There's a bathroom right down the hall you can use. I'll be right back." Without another word, he spun on his heel and strode out of the kitchen.

Still trying to get her breathing under control, Londyn cleaned up and made her way back to the kitchen. The heated interlude had left her throbbing everywhere and it took a few seconds to remember what she'd been doing. *Oh, yeah, the dough.* When he came back, she picked up their previous conversation. She needed to say something to distract her from what just happened. "Now that you know what I'm making, it's your turn to share."

"I decided on surf and turf. You mentioned having trouble with steaks, so I'm going to make you one that'll melt in your mouth." He pointed to two large lobster tails that had been cracked with the meat resting on top of the shell and skewers packed with vegetables—corn, mushrooms, green and red bell peppers, and zucchini. "We'll have these brushed with an herbed butter. All of it will be done on the grill. And since you're making French bread from scratch, I'm going to leave those store-bought ones I have in the freezer." Braxton kissed the tip of her nose. "Oh, and because you seem to have this thing with purple, for drinks, I'm going to whip up a Purple People-eater. The ingredients are a secret, so I'm not telling."

Her mouth watered and she'd concede him that one. "I think I just got hungry," she said with a smile. "While you make the ice cream, I'm going to get the cobbler and bread ready."

"Doesn't the bread have to rise a couple of times? Or at least that's what my sister always says when I beg her to make rolls."

"I did the first rise overnight in the refrigerator to save time and took it out to bring to room temperature about thirty minutes before you arrived. It should be ready to bake in about an hour."

"Sounds like a plan." Braxton took the old-fashioned crank-style ice cream maker out to the deck, layered the ice and rock salt, sealed it and rotated the arm.

Londyn stood there watching the play of muscles in his arms flex and bunch with each revolution. He glanced up, caught her staring and grinned. "That man's smile is going to get me in so much trouble," she muttered, spinning around and going back to the counter. After finishing, she opened the sliding door. "How's it coming?"

"It's getting stiff, so I think it's close to being ready. You all done?"

"Yep. Bread is rising and the cobbler's in the oven." They had worked in a relaxed domesticity reminiscent of a married couple and it gave her pause.

"Hey." Braxton touched her arm. "Where did you go?"

He had a way of looking at her with such caring that it both frightened and excited her. "I was just calculating cooking times. Did you say something?"

He shook his head and continued to scrutinize her as if he didn't believe a word she'd said.

"Is it done?"

"Let's see. I'll be back with a couple of spoons." He disappeared inside, came back in a flash and handed her a spoon. Opening the lid, he was poised to dip in his spoon when she stopped him.

"I think I should go first. I want to make sure it tastes good." Londyn scooped out a small portion of the soft cream and brought it to her mouth. She had outdone herself this time and it was all she could do not to break out in a dance. Keeping her features neutral, she gestured for him to try it.

Braxton's eyes widened and he groaned. "This is the best damn ice cream I've ever eaten."

A wide grin spread across her face. "And it's going to be even better with the peach cobbler." She wiggled her eyebrows. They repacked it so it could harden and went back inside. Londyn took a seat at the bar.

"I see I'm going to have to up my cooking game with you." He melted butter in a small bowl, added several herbs and brushed the mixture first over the vegetables, then the seafood. "Would you like some music?"

"I thought you'd never ask. I never cook without it."

He washed and dried his hands. "You should've said something earlier. What do you want to hear?"

"R&B or jazz."

"I have playlist with a mixture of both." He picked up his

phone and pressed several buttons. The sound of Maxwell's voice flowed from hidden speakers. "Come dance with me." He extended his hand and helped her off the stool.

Londyn wrapped her arms around his waist and laid her head on his chest, while he sang the words of "Fortunate" softly. As she listened to the lyrics, she agreed with the artist because she was fortunate that Braxton had come into her life. Even if things didn't work out later, she now knew how it felt to have a man treat her as if she were a priceless jewel. When the song ended, he didn't miss a beat as he swung her out and moved in rhythm to an up-tempo Boney James tune. "Where did you learn to dance so well?"

Laughing, he said, "I couldn't go to all the school dances and get on that floor and make a fool of myself. The guys *and* the girls would've teased me forever."

She giggled. "You're right. I remember how ruthless teens can be."

"They are. My niece also keeps me up to date with the latest moves. Although, some of these new dances are too much for this old body. I don't even know how they get their body parts to move like that."

He demonstrated a move that contorted his body and looked like a broken Frankenstein. Londyn doubled over laughing until tears ran down her face. "Okay, I'm done," she said, trying to catch her breath.

Braxton wasn't any better. When they finally calmed down, he kissed her temple. "Maybe we should just listen to the music instead."

"I think you might be right." She wiped the lingering moisture from the corners of her eyes. She hadn't had this much fun with a guy in... She stilled. She'd never laughed with a man this way or felt so comfortable with one, and definitely not in such a short time.

"How long does it take for the bread to cook?"

"About twenty or twenty-five minutes." She checked to see how much it had risen. "It should be ready to bake in about ten minutes." She glanced over at the oven timer. The cobbler still had another five minutes.

He angled his head. "Okay. I'm going to start the grill. Hopefully, we can have everything done close to the same time. How do you like your steak cooked?"

"Extra juicy with no pink."

With a smile and shake of his head, he left her standing there.

They sat down to eat half an hour later. Braxton turned on the fireplace. The mouth-watering aromas from the meat, vegetables and bread had her stomach growling loud enough to shake the walls.

Braxton slanted her a glance. "Does that mean you're hungry."

"Starved." Londyn rubbed her hands together. "Let's get our eat on." They filled their plates and sat at the table that Braxton had set with elegant white china that matched his gray theme, and candles. She wanted to save the steak for last, so she sampled the vegetable kabob first. The herbed butter brought out the flavors perfectly. "Mmm." The lobster was just as good. She rotated her plate, cut into the steak and popped it into her mouth. Braxton sat watching her, seemingly waiting for her verdict. "Oh, my goodness." She moaned and swooned in her chair.

He lifted a brow, but was smiling. "That good?"

"So much better than good. This is *melt-in-your-mouth, slap-your-mama good!*" She leaned forward for emphasis. "You can cook for me forever." She gasped softly. *What the hell did I just say?*

Braxton couldn't stop staring at Londyn. And he couldn't stop his thoughts from wondering "what if." She hadn't said a word since she'd made the statement and did her best not to look at him. He had been enjoying their camaraderie and didn't want it to end with her being uncomfortable. Placing his fork on his plate, he rounded the table and hunkered down next to her. "Look at me, Londyn."

Her head slowly came up. "I don't want you to think I'm trying to suggest anything because—"

He silenced her with a kiss. "The thought never crossed my mind." Somehow, when she'd said it, the words didn't hit him the way they had with Taryn, who only took, but never gave. Londyn had given him more in three weeks than all of the women in his past combined. "I tell you what, if things don't work out with us, I'll still cook for you every now and again if you promise more of those brownies and that ice cream."

Londyn gave him the smile he'd come to look for and said, "It's a deal."

"Can we go back to having fun now? I thought we were having a good time."

She caressed his cheek, then leaned down and touched her mouth to his. "We were having the best time."

The feel of her soft lips on his almost made his control slip and he thought it best that he return to his side of the table and grabbed his drink. Instead of a sip, he gulped down a good portion of it, hoping it would cool his arousal.

She picked up her glass. "By the way, this is really good. The deep purple is my favorite color." She took a sip and resumed eating. Minutes passed before she spoke again. "Okay, I need you to tell me what you did to this steak."

"Seasoned it and threw it on the grill."

Londyn narrowed her eyes. "So that's how you want to play it, huh? Well, me and my *warm* peach cobbler and *delicious* ice cream can just go home."

The sparkle was back in her eyes and her playfulness had returned. "That's playing dirty, doc."

"No dirtier than you, Mr. Harper."

Braxton held up his hands in surrender. "You win. There's no way I'm letting you leave without sampling your dessert." She smothered a giggle and he realized what he'd said. "Your peach cobbler and ice cream," he clarified. Though sampling *her* was never far from his mind. And every time he thought about what happened earlier, it made him hard. He was damn near *forty* and believed he had good control of his sexual urges, but Londyn proved him wrong each and every time they were together. She might be physically ready, but those fleeting moments of uncertainty he saw in her eyes told him, emotionally, she hadn't quite gotten there. At some point, he knew the attraction building between them would reach a boiling point. He only hoped when it did, they'd both be on the same page. He glanced up to find her staring at him expectantly. He'd been so lost in his thoughts, he almost forgot what she asked. "It all starts with a good cut of meat. If you're shopping in the grocery store, I'd go for the USDA Choice grade. It'll have more marbling, which will result in a more tender and *juicy* steak."

"Is that what this is?"

"No. This is prime grade, what you usually find in the more expensive restaurants or hotels."

"You went out of your way to do this, didn't you? Because I don't ever recall seeing that grade of meat in a regular grocery store."

Braxton didn't think of it as going out of his way. When he liked a woman—and he liked Londyn a lot—he tried to show her in whatever ways he could. "I wanted you to have a good steak."

Londyn grasped his hand and gave it a gentle squeeze. "And you did. It was the best steak I've ever had, restaurants, included. I just hope my peach cobbler doesn't bring the meal down."

"If it's as good as your brownies, it can only enhance the meal. As soon as my food settles, it's gonna be me, a big piece of cobbler and as much of that ice cream I can fit in my bowl." They cleared the table together, then he led her into the family room to relax. He brought her close to him on the sofa and draped an arm around her shoulders.

She sighed. "I'm so full right now, I could fall asleep." She rested her head against his shoulder.

"You can stretch out if you like."

"I'm fine right here."

So was he. "Do you want to watch TV?"

"Mmm, no. The music is nice," she murmured.

Braxton leaned back and closed his eyes. They didn't talk. He didn't need to say anything, content with listening to the wail of the saxophone and being with her. He couldn't recall when he'd last enjoyed a woman so much. Typically, he had a tendency to be more on the serious side, unless he was around his immediate family and his two friends. But he'd bantered and joked with Londyn as easily as if he'd done it all his life. He didn't know how much time had passed when she called his name softly.

"Braxton?"

"What is it?"

"I think I'm ready for dessert."

Chuckling, he said, "I've been ready."

Londyn lifted her head, frowned and elbowed him. "Why didn't you say something?"

"Because I was enjoying holding you in my arms." He stroked a finger down her cheek.

"So, remember what happened earlier in the kitchen?"

"You mean the kisses?"

Londyn nodded. "I think we should get off this couch before

we get into trouble." She jumped up and nearly ran to the kitchen.

Braxton rose to his feet and followed, a wide grin plastered on his face. He asked her to get bowls from a cabinet while he retrieved the ice cream churn and placed it in the sink. "Serving spoons and the ice cream scoop are in that drawer." He pointed. Londyn dished up the cobbler and before she could put the spoon in the sink, Braxton grabbed it, dug out a big spoonful and put it in his mouth. He prayed no one in his family ever asked him who made the best peach cobbler because he'd most likely never get any food from his mother and sister again. Londyn's beat theirs, hands down and he thought no one could bake as well as the women in his family. Her French bread had been amazing, as well. "I'm going to say this and, if you breathe a word of this to anyone, I'll deny it and never speak to you again. But this is better than my mom's."

"Hey, now." She snapped her fingers and did a little hip swerve.

He'd known her less than a month, but he had to find a way to keep this woman in his life.

# CHAPTER 7

"I guess I'm going to have to get used to these weeknight dinners, since your weekends are tied up with Braxton," Monique teased as she hugged Londyn.

Londyn pulled her friend into the foyer. "Oh, hush and come in. Felicia's already here."

"The only reason I came is because I want to get an update on your relationship…and because I knew you were making French bread."

Felicia poked her head out of the kitchen. "Hey, Nique. And that's why I'm here, too."

"Hey, girl." They embraced. "The bread smells so good."

Londyn placed her hands on her hips. "Both of you can just leave. And you know what? I'm not telling y'all nothing." Ignoring them, she placed slices of the bread in a basket with a small bowl of softened butter. She had decided on a salad bar with chicken, shrimp, cheeses, a variety of vegetables and bacon with a honey-lime vinaigrette for their Thursday dinner. Felicia had made mango margaritas to drink. Once they were settled at the table, Londyn asked Monique about the dinner date she'd had.

Monique rolled her eyes. "All I know is the next time my cousin tries to set me up with someone, I'm going to seriously hurt her. He's forty-one and works as a business manager and we hit it off pretty well at my cousin's house. We were supposed to go to dinner, but we ended up at one of those dinner clubs." She slanted them a glance. "For the thirty and *under* crowd. The music was so loud and obnoxious I couldn't hear myself think. He got mad because I didn't want to dance and refused to pay for the two drinks and expensive bottle of wine he ordered."

"I'm getting mad and I wasn't even there," Felicia said with disgust.

"Do you know what he said when I pointed out that *he'd* asked *me* out, not the other way around? He told me, 'you're a doctor, you can afford it.'"

Londyn's mouth fell open. "Oh, I know he didn't. What did you do?"

"Threw up the deuces, called Lyft and took my ass home," she finished with a smug smile. They dissolved in a fit of laughter.

"I would've loved to see his expression when that bill came and you were nowhere around," Londyn said, still chuckling.

Felicia wiped tears from her eyes. "Same. Did he try to call you later?"

Monique shook her head. "Not once. When I got home, I blocked his number, then called my cousin and told her she'd better not ever mention my name to another man. The good thing is I had him pick me up a block from my office, so he has no idea where I live."

"I have to wonder if he lied about his job," Londyn said, spearing a cucumber.

"I wouldn't be surprised." Monique frowned. "Enough of that. I'm trying to enjoy my bread."

"Since I haven't seen any action in at least four months, we can just skip me and go straight to Londyn." Felicia sipped her margarita. "Oh, this is good. Go ahead, girl. Spill it."

"We've only talked by text or phone for the past couple of weeks because both our schedules have been hectic." She couldn't believe it was the end of March already, and a little over a month since she'd met Braxton. It seemed like they'd known each other much longer. "But he cooked for me and, oh, my goodness, the man can *cook*!"

"Please tell me has at least one brother."

"Sorry, Felicia. He only has an older sister."

"What about friends? I figure he wouldn't be hanging out with scrubs."

She smiled. "He mentioned a couple of guys, but I have no idea whether they're married or not."

"Two? That means one for you and one for me, Felicia."

"You two are so crazy."

"Can he bring it in the bedroom?"

Of the three friends, Felicia was the most uninhibited and good sex had been part of her criteria for as long as Londyn could remember. *No sense wasting time with a man who can't curl your toes or at least make you wet,* she'd always said. "We haven't gotten that far yet." Not for lack of chemistry. The fact that he'd brought her to orgasm while she was fully clothed told her he'd definitely be able to bring it—and then some. Somehow, he'd been able to detect that small part of her that was still broken, that still feared she wouldn't measure up when it came to sex.

"Have you at least kissed the man?"

"Yep." She couldn't hide her smile.

"Aw, sookie, sookie. Look at that smile. Braxton's lip love must be on point," Monique said, grinning.

Her eyes drifted closed. "He's a great guy—generous, attentive—and there's something about him that has my pulse racing and, at the same time, makes me feel protected." Londyn opened her eyes and found Felicia and Monique staring at her. "What?"

"You're falling in love with him," Monique said.

"It's hard to keep from falling for a man who treats me as if I'm special." She would never forget how he'd eased her embarrassment when she accidentally made the comment about forever. Any other man would have accused her of trying to push him to the altar. His promise to cook for her even if what they had didn't last still resonated with her. She most likely wouldn't think about holding him to it, but it was nice of him to offer.

Felicia grasped Londyn's hand. "I truly hope this works out for you guys. You deserve to be happy."

"Me, too. But if it doesn't…" She shrugged.

"When's the next date?"

"We're going to the movies tomorrow. I have to admit, this is the first time I've been with a man who plans dates down to the smallest detail. But I think it's part of his personality." Londyn had also noticed that Braxton appeared to think more than he talked, and he was far more organized than her. And Londyn considered herself to be very orderly.

"I would think so with his career. Working with computer networks requires organizational, analytical, and critical thinking skills," Felicia noted. "Are you saying he's boring?"

"Not at all. We have a great time together."

"And you're going to have a better time once you do the do with him."

She threw a carrot at Felicia. "Is that all you think about?"

"What?" she asked with a laugh. "I'm just going by the vibes you're giving off, and if you sit here and say you haven't thought about it at least once, lightning is going to strike your butt."

Monique scooted her chair away. "Let me get out of the line of fire."

Londyn tried to maintain a glare, but failed. "I can't stand y'all."

"That's what I thought," Felicia said, lifting her glass in mock toast.

They finished eating while laughing. Felicia and Monique were a pain in the butt sometimes, but Londyn loved her girls and she didn't know what she'd do without them. She overrode their protests to help clean up and walked them to the door.

"Thanks for dinner and find out if those two friends are single. Nique and I will be happy to do a triple date."

Monique shook her head. "After that last one, I don't know, girl. I might need some time to myself to get over that fiasco."

Londyn hugged them both. "Be safe."

"I will," they chorused.

Smiling, she returned to the kitchen. It took her a quarter of an hour to restore it to its former state. She turned off all the lights and walked down the short hallway to her bedroom. The light was blinking on her cell, indicating messages. Her parents had emailed a few photos of them on the beach and on one of the tours they'd taken. Their faces held so much joy. They had worked hard and deserved this time. She deleted the two spam emails. Braxton had sent a text an hour ago to see if she'd decided on a movie. She had narrowed her choices to two and sent the reply. When she had initially suggested they play it by ear and select one once there, he'd countered with sending her the movie selections for three nearby theaters. Londyn got the feeling that he didn't do much on the fly. A thought popped into her mind. It was time to shake things up.

Friday afternoon, Braxton sat at his desk thinking about Londyn. It had only been two weeks since their dinner, but he'd missed spending time with her. She 'd gotten under his skin so effortlessly, reminding him how monotonous his life had become.

Outside of work, spending time with his family and two friends, Braxton's routine rarely varied. Each week looked exactly the same. Although, as of late, he, Cole and Axel had started canceling their weekly meet ups because they each had found that potentially special woman. He just hoped none of their newly established relationships ended in heartbreak. Especially his own. Londyn had danced herself into his life and was steadily working her way into his heart. He tried to rationalize that they'd only known each other a month, that he couldn't be falling in love in such a short period of time. Apparently, his heart hadn't gotten the memo because everything in him said she was the one. Logic had ruled his life up to this point. However, he had a strong feeling that this time would be different. Rotating toward his computer, he checked his schedule. His last appointment had been canceled, which meant he could leave a little earlier.

Braxton picked up a folder and a brochure from the center where Londyn worked fell out. Once again, his mind traveled to his past. After talking with her, he'd googled pornography and sexual addictions and got the shock of his life. While he had never progressed to that level, reading all the information cleared up a lot of things for him. It had taken an old college classmate's obsession to change Braxton. The guy had wanted to celebrate the end of senior year with a movie marathon. After less than an hour, Braxton left and never watched another adult film again. That had been almost fifteen years ago, and the urge had not come back. For that he was grateful.

His cell buzzed. Seeing Tonya's name on the display sent a chill down his spine. His niece never called him during a work-day. "Hey, baby girl."

"Happy birthday, Uncle Braxton," Tonya sang.

He let out a sigh of relief. "Thank you, baby girl. But what are you doing calling me at work? You almost gave me a heart attack."

She giggled. "Oops, I'm sorry. Can you come over tonight? I made you a cake."

"I appreciate that, Tonya." He didn't want to cancel his date, but he didn't want to offend Tonya, either. "I have plans for tonight, but I can come by early tomorrow, and you can sing and everything." She had inherited her father's off-key voice, but she sang with so much enthusiasm that no one had the heart to tell her.

"Do you have a date?"

"Yes."

"*Really?* Mom, guess what? Uncle Braxton has a date tonight," she yelled.

Braxton scrubbed a hand down his face. *Great.* "Tonya, why are you calling for your mother?"

"So, little brother has a date, huh? That's what I call a great birthday present."

"Hey, sis. I was telling Tonya I could come by tomorrow for the cake."

"She's going to a sleepover later tonight for the weekend. Can you just stop by for a minute around seven? You don't have to stay long and you can even bring your date. We'll sing, you blow out the candles, then you two can be on your way. It wouldn't happen to be the woman you were dancing with at the wedding, would it?" Debra asked slyly.

"What makes you think it's her?"

"I *saw* you on the dance floor with her, Braxton. You were totally into her. Now, answer the question."

"Yes," he muttered.

"So, you'll come."

"Yeah, I'll stop by for a few minutes." What else could he say?

"I can't wait to meet your date. See you later."

Disconnecting, he groaned inwardly. He didn't think he and Londyn had reached the meet-the-family stage yet. But he couldn't disappoint his niece, either. She'd had him wrapped around her little finger since birth. And if his mother got wind of it... He groaned again. Braxton picked up the phone and sent a text to Londyn asking if she minded a short stop before their movie. He deliberately didn't mention his birthday. For him, it was just another day and he didn't need a celebration.

As he powered down his computer an hour later, Londyn's reply came through: *Sure. No problem.*

Braxton had enough time to shower and change into jeans, a long-sleeved tee and boots before picking up Londyn. When she came toward him wearing body-hugging black jeans and an off-the-shoulder fitted gray top, with a sexy runway strut, he was glad he'd suggested meeting in the lobby. Had he gone up to her place, he wouldn't have left until he had touched, kissed and tasted every inch of her body. "Hey, baby."

"Hi, yourself," Londyn said, coming up on tiptoe to meet his kiss. Hand-in-hand, they walked out to his car. "Both movies start after eight, and with all the advertisements at the beginning, we should have more than enough time to go by your sister's house."

"Hopefully, it won't take long." However, knowing his sister, she'd find a way to delay them leaving until she finished her interrogation. "How was your week?"

"Long," she said with a chuckle. "I'm glad it's the weekend."

"Same here." They'd acquired two more projects and he'd taken up the slack because the other architect still hadn't returned from his leave. They passed the thirty-minute drive conversing quietly interspersed with moments of silence while music played softly. Braxton parked in front of his sister's house and debated whether to ask Londyn to wait, but his sister appeared in the doorway before he could utter a word.

Londyn shifted in her seat to face him. "If I didn't know better, I'd think you didn't want me to meet your family."

He studied her. She was right in a way, but not for the reasons she most likely assumed. "That's not it at all. I just don't want you to be uncomfortable. Remember what I told you at the wedding?"

"About your mom trying to marry you off? Yes."

"My sister is the same way and they both can be a little... overzealous. I'd rather be the one to decide the direction of my relationship with you *without* any interference from my family."

A small smile curved her lips. "And have you decided the direction of this relationship?"

"Yes, and I'd be more than happy to show you anytime you want." Despite his sister watching from the porch, he leaned over and slanted his mouth over Londyn's in a deep provocative kiss, willing her to feel just where he wanted them to go. "Any other questions?"

She cleared her throat. "Oo-*kay*. Um...so no. We should probably get out before your sister comes over."

Braxton sent an unhurried glance over to where Debra stood. Thankfully, the darkness and his tinted windows prevented his sister from seeing them clearly. "You're right." He went around to her side to help her out and then started up the walkway. He kissed Debra's cheek. "Hey, sis. This is Londyn. Londyn, my sister Debra."

"It's really nice to meet you, Londyn," Debra said with a bright smile.

"Nice meeting you, too."

"You guys come on in." She held the door open.

"*Surprise!*"

Braxton froze. He met his mother's smiling face and wanted to flee.

"*Happy birthday to you,*" the group standing in his sister's living room sang boisterously.

"I am so gonna get you," he whispered to Debra.

She merely smiled and kept singing.

He glanced down at the amused smile on Londyn's face as

she joined in the refrain. Loud applause and whistles sounded as the last note faded away.

"I take it today's your birthday. Happy birthday." Londyn gave his hand a reassuring squeeze.

"Yes and thank you. I'm sorry, I didn't know she was going to do this."

"It wouldn't have been a surprise if you did," she said wryly.

"I like you, Londyn," Debra said, laughing. "Come meet the family."

Debra—" Braxton released a deep sigh when Debra whisked Londyn off.

"Happy birthday, old man," Cole said, his arm firmly around Malaya's waist.

"Happy birthday, Braxton," Malaya repeated, leaning up to kiss his cheek.

"Thanks." Braxton hoped the fact that she had come with Cole meant that things were changing in his friend's favor.

Axel clapped Braxton on the shoulder and smiled. "Happy birthday."

He eyed Axel and Cole. "How is I talked to both of you last week and neither of you mentioned this?"

"Hey, your mom and sister promised bodily harm if we said anything," Axel said, raising a hand.

He grunted. "I thought you guys canceled the Friday night get-together because you had something else to do?"

Chuckling, Cole said, "I did. Coming to your surprise birthday party. Is that Londyn?"

"Yeah. We were supposed to go to the movies." Braxton shifted his gaze to where his sister stood introducing Londyn to their mother.

"Guess that's not happening tonight," Axel said. "And unfortunately, I can't stay all night."

"Why not?"

"You know why not."

Braxton nodded. "Oh, that's right, because Friday nights are reserved for Naphressa."

Axel shrugged. "It is what it is."

He opened his mouth to say something else, but saw that his mother had that pleased smile on her face and Londyn in an arm lock. "I'll be right back. I need to rescue Londyn from Mom before she scares her." His long strides covered the distance in a few seconds. "Hey, Mom." He placed a kiss on her upturned cheek.

"Happy Birthday, baby. I can't believe you haven't brought Londyn to visit. She was just telling me about her job. I think it's wonderful that she's able to help people who need counseling. You should bring her to the family dinner."

Braxton saw Londyn's eyes widen and knew it was time to get away. "Mom, I want to introduce Londyn to a few more people. Thanks for the party." He grabbed Londyn's hand and nearly dragged her across the room and into the kitchen. Placing his hands on her shoulders, he pulled her close. "Are you alright?"

"I'm fine. Your family is really nice." She eased back and searched his face. "The question is are *you* alright? You look slightly bothered."

He ran a hand over his close-cropped hair. "I just wasn't expecting all...all this." He gestured toward the family room.

She folded her arms. "What you really mean is that you need to have everything planned down to the minute detail and this threw your schedule right out the window."

"That's not true."

"No? When was the last time you gave in to wild impulse or allowed yourself to be spontaneous?"

Braxton didn't answer because he couldn't. And how had she read him so easily? "Is this an official diagnosis, Dr. Grant?"

Londyn shook her head. "I don't need a degree to figure you out." She hugged him. "You just hit the big four O. New decade, new attitude. It's okay to do something spur-of-the-moment occasionally, baby. Your family went through all this trouble to celebrate you, so let's go enjoy it. We can postpone our movie date until next weekend."

*Baby?* Braxton's heart skipped a beat. "Am I your baby?"

"I think I'd like you to be my baby," she said with a shy smile.

"Well, I *know* I want you to be mine." He kissed her. "You're good for me, Londyn."

"I'm finding you're the same for me, too."

Taking her hand, he led her back to the party. "I'd like you to meet my friends, Axel, Cole, and Malaya." They all greeted each other and Londyn struck up a conversation with Malaya.

"She seems like cool people." Cole said, quietly.

"She is." And Braxton was falling in love with her.

# CHAPTER 8

Saturday evening, Londyn zipped and buttoned her jeans, then pulled on a pair of low-heel ankle boots. Braxton would be picking her up for their postponed movie date shortly. His reaction to the birthday party had been on her mind all week. After their talk in the kitchen, he'd loosened up and enjoyed himself, but in her estimation, he needed to learn to go with the flow sometimes. It was time to help her baby—and he was definitely her baby—let go. A smile flitted around her mouth and she grabbed her phone.

She was still smiling when Braxton arrived. "Hi." Braxton kissed her until she melted against him. When she opened her eyes, he had that pleased male smile.

"Hey, beautiful. Ready?"

"Yes." He helped her into her jacket.

"Which movie did you decide on?"

"Actually, I didn't."

Braxton stared at her, obviously confused. "Okay," he said slowly. "What exactly does that mean?"

She looped her arm in his. "It means I want to do something

different, something reckless and impulsive." Myriad expressions crossed his face. "Trust me."

"I do." He didn't say anything for a moment and she could feel his struggle. "Okay, what did you have in mind?"

Giving him a winning smile, Londyn said, "You'll see."

"Londyn, I'm going to need directions, or at least an address."

"No you won't because I'm driving." Londyn held up her keys. "And if you say one thing about not allowing a woman to drive, you'll never see that peach cobbler and ice cream again." She punctuated each word with a poke in his chest.

He chuckled and gently took hold of her hand. "That's hitting pretty low, but I'm going to go along with it because I *need* that cobbler. And I need you," he added, his eyes locked on hers.

She could barely breathe and her heart pounded hard against her chest. If she hadn't already been falling in love with him, his words tonight would have pushed her over the edge.

"Now, Dr. Grant, I want you to write in your therapy notes that I'm going to be spontaneous and like it."

"Noted, Mr. Harper." She made a show of writing on an imaginary pad. They burst out laughing and continued the good-natured ribbing all the way down to the parking garage.

Braxton let out a low whistle when they stopped at her Kona Blue Mustang Shelby GT350. "Nice ride."

"Thank you. I love it." She grown up dreaming of owning the car. Her parents had given her the car on her thirty-fifth birthday, saying that they were proud of all of her accomplishments and wanted to reward Londyn for all her hard work.

"I don't know why, but I never pictured you driving something like this."

"Why?" Londyn asked, sliding into the driver's seat.

"You seem so prim and proper most times."

"Ha! I'm prim and proper Monday through Friday from

eight to five, after that, I let my hair down figuratively and literally." Putting the stick into gear she drove out of the garage and hit the road in a burst of speed.

"Whoa. Don't you think you're driving a little fast?'

"This isn't fast. I can show you fast, if you like," she said sweetly, leaning toward him and batting her eyelashes. She refocused on the road and smiled at him muttering about women and speed demons. She merged onto I-75N and half an hour later parked in the lot of Andretti Indoor Karting & Games in Marietta.

Braxton eyed her suspiciously. "What are you planning?"

"I'm planning on us having lots of fun. It's time to let that inner kid out again." Londyn hopped out of the car and headed for the entrance. The sounds of cars racing, bowling pins crashing and lively chatter greeted them.

"Go Karts?"

"Yep. Have you been here before?"

"No, and I haven't driven one in over twenty years."

"Well, tonight's the perfect time to dust off the cobwebs."

He just shook his head and grinned. "Okay, let's have some fun."

They decided on the upstairs track, designed with more straightaways for less experienced drivers. Londyn was pleased to see Braxton's competitive spirit come alive as they challenged each other round and round the track. Whizzing past the karts and hitting the curves made her feel exhilarated, much like she did when she was with Braxton.

At the end, Braxton helped her out of the go kart. "That was fun. What's next?"

"Can you bowl?"

He shrugged. "I might be able to do a little something."

She lifted a brow. "Alrighty now. You think you've got game?"

He tossed her a bold wink. "Only one way to find out."

His quiet reflective side had captured her attention, but seeing this more carefree version of him caused Londyn to lose even more of her heart. She'd vowed not to fall in love again, didn't want to risk being hurt and she'd broken that promise. As she'd told her friends, it was hard not to fall for a man like Braxton.

Braxton rented a lane for them and after getting shoes and finding the right balls, the competition began. "Ladies first."

She made sure her stance was correct and sent the ball sailing down the lane. And straight into the gutter. She spun around and pointed a finger his way. "Not one word."

"I didn't say anything." He tried to hide his smile, brought his hand up and pantomimed zipping his lips.

Londyn managed to pick up six pins on a spare. When Braxton stood, her gaze was glued to his firm butt in those jeans. She had never thought about a man being sexy while bowling, but this man had proved her wrong. His thighs and biceps flexed with every move, and his sensual, deliberate steps had her fantasizing about those same movements in her bed. The sound of pins flying everywhere jerked her out of her thoughts. She peered around him. Of course, he'd walked right up and gotten a strike. "Lucky," she grumbled and got up to take her turn. This time she, too, got one.

"Okay, okay, the girl's got a little game."

The next time when he got up the two women in the next lane stopped what they were doing and stared at him. For the first time in her life, Londyn felt jealousy coursing through her veins.

"Londyn, it's your turn." Braxton touched her arm.

"What?"

"It's your turn." Curving his arm around her waist, he said, "How about a kiss for luck?"

"For me or you?"

"Does it matter?"

"Not one iota." He brushed a short kiss over her lips, but she wasn't done. Pulling his head down, she took charge of the kiss, swirling her tongue around his until she heard his soft groan.

Braxton broke off the kiss. "You keep that up and these people are going to get an eyeful." He lifted his head. "Too late."

She took a quick glance around and saw a number of people watching them. *What has gotten into me? I do not kiss men in public.* Backing out of his embrace, she picked up her ball. It took all her concentration to get it down the lane. After that impromptu kiss, Londyn's game went steadily downhill and she barely made it to a hundred points. Braxton, on the other hand, performed as if he'd been bowling for years.

"Aw, don't be mad, sweetheart. I'll let you win next time," he teased.

Londyn elbowed him in the side. "Whatever." His warm laughter flowed around her and calmed her irritation.

"Let's go get something to eat."

They returned the shoes, stopped at the bathroom to wash their hands and made their way over to the grill. "I'm not that hungry," she said, checking out the menu. "Are you opposed to sharing an appetizer?"

"No. The Andretti Platter looks good."

She read the description—potato skins, quesadilla, spinach artichoke dip with tortilla chips and several dipping sauces. "This works for me. And I'll have a lemonade."

He gave the order and chose the same for his drink. "Thanks for tonight." He stared at her intently and his voice dropped an octave. 'It's been awhile since I've had this much fun and I'm looking forward to doing it again."

"I'm glad you enjoyed yourself." His gaze warmed her from the inside out and it took everything she had not to fan herself. She needed a minute because, right now, she wanted him with everything in her. He'd said she would be able to determine the perfect time for them to take their relationship to the next step. Londyn was more than ready.

The combination of seeing Londyn's jeans stretch taut across her round backside every time she bent over while bowling and her licking sauce off her fingers had Braxton near the end of his control. It also didn't help watching her work the gear shift in her car. Every time she shifted, she had a habit of caressing the stick, causing him to grow harder and harder.

"Oh, my goodness, that was great." Londyn dropped down on her sofa and leaned her head back. "Can I get you something?"

*Yes. You naked in your bed.* "No, I'm good." He lowered himself next to her.

She reached for her iPad on the table and powered it on. "I need some music." Moments later, the distinctive sound of Prince sounded throughout the room. "Ooh, this is my song."

*You have got to be kidding me.* Braxton wasn't going to make it, not with the refrain of "Do Me, Baby" running through his head. And *definitely* not with her singing the chorus—eyes closed, head thrown back, and arms in the air. He shifted in his seat to relieve the pressure in his groin and stripped off his jacket.

She must have noticed something in his expression because she asked, "You don't like this song?"

"The song's fine. It's just that I don't need any reminders about… I mean, it's sort of suggestive."

Angling her head his way, she gave him a sensual smile. "Hmm, you're right." She straddled his lap, gyrating against him. "And what do you plan to do about that suggestion?"

Braxton gritted his teeth and his breathing increased. "Londyn, you're playing with fire, sweetheart. I'm doing my best to wait until you're ready, but you're killing me."

Londyn trailed kisses along his jaw and whispered in his ear, "Obviously, you're not hearing what I'm telling you."

His hands clamped down on her hips to still her movements. He was close to exploding, but needed to hear her say it. He searched her gaze for any indecision or hesitation, but only saw raw desire. "I need you to tell me what you want."

Her eyes met his. "You, Braxton. I want you, and I want you to do me exactly how the song says...until I—"

Groaning, he crushed his mouth to hers, cutting off her erotic plea. He leaped to his feet with her in his arms. "Bedroom."

"Hallway. Straight back." He entered her bedroom and placed her on her feet, then waited as she turned on the lamp beside her bed.

She sauntered back to where Braxton still stood and removed her shoes. Her hands went to her sweater, but he placed a staying hand on hers.

"I've got this tonight. You can strip for me next time." Braxton felt and saw her stiffen. "What is it, Londyn? If you've changed your mind, it's okay."

Londyn shook her head. "I haven't."

*Something's going on with her.* He knew felt it as surely as his own heartbeat. Suddenly, it finally hit him. She'd been hurt by a man—and badly—if the snatches of fear and sadness she displayed on occasion were any indication. He cursed under his breath. Picking her up, he placed her in the center of the bed, then followed her down. "Do you know how beautiful you are?" he murmured, placing light kisses on her forehead, eyelids, nose and cheeks, before taking her mouth in another heated kiss. His hand searched under her top and caressed her bare skin.

She sucked in a deep breath. "Hurry, Braxton."

"I can't do that. You're the woman I've been waiting for and I plan to take my time touching, tasting, kissing, *doing* each and every part of your body." Slowly, methodically, he divested her of her clothes, lingering in each spot and attempting to convey just how much he wanted her. Braxton couldn't heal her, but he would do his best to make her forget every man in her past and remember only him and the pleasure they shared. Cupping her breasts in his hands, he kneaded and massaged them before bending to take one nipple in his mouth. She moaned loudly. He released one breast and kissed the other while his hand traveled down her flat belly to the softness between her thighs.

Londyn cried out and arched off the bed. She pushed his shirt up and over his head. Her hands roamed purposely over his chest and arms, making his muscles contract and flex beneath her touch. "You're beautiful, too."

His soft laughter turned to a moan when hands moved lower and cupped him through his jeans. Braxton was nearing the end of his control. Rolling off the bed, he quickly shed the rest of his clothes and donned a condom. He kissed his way up her body until she lay beneath him, loving the feel of her soft curves against his body. He used his hands and mouth to tease and torment, taking her to the brink of ecstasy, time and time again, her passionate cries filling the room.

"Brax…Braxton." She moaned and writhed as his hand feathered down her thigh, then back up to her core.

"Is this how you want me to do you?" Braxton parted her sensitive folds, slid one finger inside and she came with a strangled cry. He added another finger, moving them in and out and prolonging the pleasure. Withdrawing his fingers, he spread her legs with his knees, his eyes never leaving hers as he slowly pushed his erection into her, inch by exquisite inch, until he was buried deep inside her. He moaned deep in his throat at the pleasure of her tight walls squeezing him. Her eyes drifted closed. "Londyn, sweetheart, look at me."

Londyn's eyes fluttered open.

"This is not just sex. This is a man making love to the woman he's falling for."

She closed her eyes and a tear escaped. "Thank you. I needed to know that it isn't because I want more with you."

Her words were like music to his ears. He pulled out to the tip and plunged deep. A shudder racked his body as he started to move in slow insistent circles. He delved deeper with each rhythmic push and Londyn wrapped her legs around him, lifting her hips to meet each thrust. The sounds of their breathing increased and he set a pace that had the bed rocking. "I knew it would be this way with us," he said. "I can't get enough of you." Braxton tilted her hips higher, never missing a beat. "I need to be deeper inside you, baby."

She clutched his shoulders. "I can't hold on," she panted, her legs tightening around his back. Grabbing the back of his head, she thrust her tongue into his mouth. He gripped her hips tighter and his strokes came faster. Abruptly, she broke off the kiss and let out a high-pitched scream as she climaxed all around him, her feminine muscles clenching him tight.

Braxton was on the verge of exploding, but didn't want to release just yet. He slowed the pace, thrusting with long, languid strokes, slowly rebuilding her passion.

"Braxton, I don't think I can take much more. *Please*."

Braxton plunged deeper and faster. Her whimpers and cries of passion excited him in a way he had never experienced and couldn't explain. He gritted his teeth, feeling her nails biting into the skin on his back, but didn't slow.

"*Braxton!*" She stiffened, then let out a scream that made the hairs stand up on the back of his neck. Her body shook, and her inner muscles contracted, clamping around him like a vise.

He threw back his head and exploded in a rush of pleasure that tore through him like a crack of lightning. His eyes slid closed, he groaned her name and shuddered above her as the spasms racked his body. He collapsed on her, and then shifted to his side, taking her with him. *This is what I've been missing all my life.* Braxton idly stroked her back while waiting for his breathing to return to normal.

"I think I've been done now," Londyn said tiredly.

So had he. In more ways than one.

# CHAPTER 9

"*Y*ou've been humming that song for the past half hour," Felicia said, staring at Londyn.

Londyn paused opening the large box filled with deodorant. "You know I love Prince."

"Yeah, but he has a catalogue of music—"Little Red Corvette", "Purple Rain", "Te Amo Corazón." Need I go on? But the only thing I've heard you singing is "Do Me Baby", and with a goofy smile on your face. So, either you've scored coveted tickets to some hologram performance of Prince or you and Braxton finally did it."

*Busted!* She had no idea that she'd been singing the song. It had been two weeks since that night with Braxton and she hadn't been able to get the lyrics out of her mind. She still couldn't believe she'd been so bold. The memory of his mouth all over her body started a low pulsing in her center and she closed her eyes briefly, willing it to stop.

"I'm waiting, Miss Thang."

Londyn glanced over her shoulder to find Felicia standing on the other side of the room with her hands on her hips. "The latter one."

A smile broke out on Felicia's face and she pumped her fist in the air. "*Yes!* Was it the hot, sweaty get-your-freak-on sex?" she asked eagerly.

"No. More like the sweet, passionate, he-stole-my-heart kind of *love-making*." Braxton had said it was more than just sex to him and she had felt it with every touch and kiss. "It's weird, but he is so different in a good way."

Felicia brought a hand to her mouth. "I don't believe it," she whispered. "Monique was right. You *are* in love with him. Have you told him about what happened with Antoine?"

"*No*," Londyn said incredulously. "And I don't plan to tell him. It's bad enough that I know." She was afraid Braxton would look at her differently and wonder how she could have allowed herself to get caught up with a man who'd taken advantage of her sexually and emotionally.

She came and sat on the floor next to Londyn. "You really need to tell him, Londyn. He shouldn't have to compete with those bad memories whenever they show up."

Her friend had a point. There had been times when she had nightmares about all the things Antoine put her through, all the promises of him doing better, and all the lies and excuses when he didn't. But his blaming her for his problems had crushed her emotionally and only recently had she finally climbed out of the abyss of pain. Everything was going well with Braxton and what she felt for him went well beyond what she had experienced in her past relationships. Londyn wanted it, no *needed* it to stay that way. Besides, she hadn't had any issues with them being intimate, so she figured she'd finally laid her past to rest. "I'll think about it." Changing the subject, she asked, "How many of these care packages are you doing?"

"*We're* doing three hundred. It would've gone so much faster if Monique were here." Monique had gone out of town for the weekend.

"I agree." She scanned Felicia's family room filled with boxes and boxes of everything from toiletries and towels to blankets and first aid supplies. "There is no way we'll finish this today. And I'm going over to my parents' house for dinner. They just returned from their trip. But I can come back tomorrow to help finish."

"Thanks. Now I don't have to stay up all night to do it. We want to distribute the tote bags next Saturday." In addition to her day job, Felicia ran a non-profit organization that provided assistance to low-income and homeless populations.

"Well, let's get busy."

The two women worked for another hour opening boxes and separating items so that they would be easy to bag tomorrow before Londyn said her goodbyes and drove to her parents' house.

"Oh, it's so good to see you," her mother said, when she opened the door to Londyn.

Londyn hugged her. "You look great, Mom. A month in the Caribbean was just what you and Dad needed."

"I've already started planning for our next trip," she said with a little laugh. "Of course, your father keeps saying I should at least let us unpack first before I book another one."

"I wish I could take off a month and go somewhere, anywhere." They entered the family room where Londyn's father sat in his favorite recliner watching a sports channel. "Hi, Dad."

He got up as fast as his sixty-nine-year-old body allowed and engulfed her in a big hug. "Hey, baby girl." He held her away from him and studied her. "Everything going okay?"

She smiled. "Yes." Better than okay. It had been a long time since she could answer his typical question truthfully.

Her father pressed a kiss to her forehead. "That's what I like to hear." He retook his seat.

"I know you took lots of pictures and I can't wait to see them."

"I'll show them to you while I'm finishing dinner," her mother said, walking toward the kitchen.

Londyn followed and sat flipping through the photos on the iPad Paulette had handed her. At sixty-six and five feet, eight inches tall, her mother had maintained her slim figure. The height gene had totally skipped Londyn, as she'd inherited her paternal grandmother's petite stature. "These are so gorgeous, especially the beach shots. I'd give anything to be sitting on one right now."

Paulette paused in stirring a pot. "Oh? I thought you said everything at work is going well." She frowned and replaced the lid. "That young man you were seeing hasn't done anything to hurt you, has he?" She came over and sat next to Londyn.

Londyn recognized the protective tone in her mother's voice. Smiling, she said, "No, and we're still seeing each other. I was only thinking I'd like to take a vacation is all." She tried not to squirm under her mother's scrutiny.

"Hmm, I see."

"See what?"

"That you've fallen in love with Braxton. I can see it in your face. You look more relaxed and there's a peace there that hasn't been in a long time."

*Why did mothers know everything?* All her life Londyn wondered how her mother could look at her and know every detail of her heart. She lowered her head and continued scrolling through the pictures.

Her mother patted her hand. "It's okay to fall in love, sweetheart. You never shared with us the details of why you ended your engagement with Antoine, but I know he hurt you. You've kept your heart locked away and your father and I have been worried you'd never open it again. I'm happy that you've found someone who makes you happy."

Londyn slowly lifted her head. She had been too ashamed to tell them what happened, and afraid her father, who had always protected her, would do Antoine bodily harm. She'd only told Felicia and Monique and, even then, Londyn hadn't shared the full extent of her trauma with them. They were her best friends and had cried with her and stayed with her when she'd taken off a week from work because she'd become so depressed she couldn't get out of bed. But Braxton was different. "Mom, Braxton is incredible, and he always makes me feel like I'm special, Like I'm an important part of his life."

"That's how it should always be, Londyn. Even if you have a disagreement. Have you told him how you feel?"

"No. I don't know if he feels the same way, and I'd rather not put my heart out there just yet." In her relationships, she had always been the first one to acknowledge her feelings and, each time, it had backfired. She knew Braxton cared for her, his actions said so. He'd even mentioned her being the woman he'd been waiting for falling for her. But until she was absolutely sure he felt the same, she planned to keep her mouth closed.

"Love carries a risk, and as a psychologist, you know that better than most. Don't let your past and what you hear every day from those struggling in their relationships determine how you live your life."

"I thought I was the psychologist," she said with a laugh.

Paulette waved a hand. "I'm a mom. It's the same thing."

"Ain't that the truth," Londyn muttered. They both laughed.

"Seriously, baby, your heart will know whether or not Braxton is the one for you. Just promise me you won't close your heart to love."

"I'm trying, Mom."

"Good. I hope we have a chance to meet him soon." She stood. "Let your father know dinner is ready."

Londyn left to deliver the message and to wash her hands before joining her parents at the dining room table. "This smells so good, Mom." Although they had flown home the previous evening, her mother had prepared a meal of barbecue chicken, potato salad, green beans and her light-as-air biscuits.

Dwight blessed the food. "Baby, you've outdone yourself. Don't get me wrong. I enjoyed our vacation, but there's nothing like coming home to one of your meals."

Her mother blushed and giggled like a schoolgirl. "Thank you, honey. I just thought a nice, home-cooked meal would be nice after eating in restaurants for a month."

Londyn held up a chicken wing. "And any time I don't have to cook, is good for me." Laughter flowed around the table.

Halfway through dinner, her father asked, "When are we going to meet this young man you're dating?"

She shot a quick glance at her mother. "I don't know yet. We've only known each other a couple of months."

"I'd only known your father six weeks before he proposed," her mother said sweetly.

Londyn had heard more than once about their whirlwind romance when they'd met during their residency, her father in his fourth and her mother in her first. Though they married right away, it wasn't until they'd begun their careers did they have Londyn. "That's not how things work these days."

"That's because you young people approach relationships with your minds and not your hearts," Paulette countered. "You're all so busy wondering if it's the right time in your careers, reading these newfangled books on finding the right mate and dating two and three people at a time, talking about you need to see which one is best, all the while ignoring blaring red flags," she ranted, shaking her head. She pinned Londyn with a stare. "All you need to do is use some common sense and trust your heart."

She couldn't dispute one word her mother said because she'd agonized over the timing with her career and her biological clock. And she finally admitted to herself that she had ignored several red flags with Antoine, particularly when it came to intimacy. Once they became engaged, he started demanding sex more often, and whenever she didn't want it, he turned into someone she didn't know. Londyn pushed down the ugly memories and let the image of Braxton's heated, but tender, kisses all over her body fill her mind and her heart instead. She just prayed he didn't change.

∾

"You sure I can't convince you to come with me to my parent's house for dinner this afternoon?" Braxton asked Londyn. His mother had called him that morning with a reminder to ask Londyn to Sunday dinner.

"Aw, that's so sweet of your mom to offer. I'd love to, but I promised my friend I'd help her finish putting together the care totes her non-profit organization will be giving out next weekend."

"What kind of organization?"

"They focus on providing resources for the low-income and homeless populations. These bags will have toiletries, blankets, socks, snacks and a few other things."

"Let me know when she's planning to do something like this again. I'd like to donate." He recognized how blessed he was and always tried to find ways to help others, particularly young African American boys. Braxton volunteered his time coaching summer sports leagues and sponsored a technology camp.

Londyn chuckled. "I'll tell Felicia, but you might be sorry. She will definitely take you up on your offer."

"I'm never sorry when it comes to these kinds of things. Now back to you joining me for dinner. What if I throw in another meal at my place?"

"Ooh, that's *so* tempting, but I'll have to take a raincheck. Your family is great and they love you, so you'll be fine."

"I don't think so. I'd enjoy it a lot more if I didn't have to listen to my mom fussing when she finds out you won't be there." Londyn was the first woman he actually wanted to bring to a family gathering. At his party, he had watched her charm his mother and father, and Debra had texted days later to tell him how much she'd liked Londyn. They liked her and he'd fallen in love with her.

"You can place the blame on me," she said. "I'll make it up to you."

"Now, that sounds like an interesting proposition. Do I get to decide how you make it up to me?" If it were up to him, they'd have a repeat of the night they'd made love.

"Hmm…depends. I'm sure we could work something out."

Braxton felt himself growing hard. Since they had started dating, he'd been in a constant state of arousal. All it took was a simple thought. "We can discuss it when I call you tonight."

"Sounds like a plan. Enjoy dinner."

He grunted.

She laughed. "I'll talk to you later."

He disconnected and tapped the phone against his chin. He had been tempted to tell her that he loved her, but decided to wait. The first time she heard the words of his heart should be done in person. He sat there a while longer contemplating how and when to tell her. It didn't surprise Braxton in the least that the idea of marriage slipped into his thoughts, as well. He'd figure it all out, but for now, he had to deal with his mother. If he were lucky, once he told her Londyn's reason, she'd let the matter drop.

Two hours later, Braxton found out that he was wrong. Dead wrong.

She opened the door excitedly and promptly looked behind him and asked, "Where's Londyn?"

"I'm your son. I can't even get a hello first before you start?"

"Hi, son. Now why didn't you invite her?"

He sighed in exasperation. "I did, but she already had plans to help a friend."

"Oh," she said, her excitement waning considerably.

"You know, I think my feelings are hurt. I thought you loved me." He gave her his best sad face.

She swatted at his arm. "Come on in here, boy."

Laughing, he kissed her cheek and followed her inside where his father and his sister's family sat around laughing and talking. He greeted everyone, then took a seat on the sofa next to his niece.

She promptly laid her head on his shoulder. "Uncle Braxton, when can we spend the night with you again? Mom said you're busy now and we shouldn't bug you about coming over."

"Tonya." His sister gave her daughter a look of warning from the kitchen where she stood helping their mother place the food on serving platters. "We've already talked about this. Your uncle has a new lady friend and he can't spend all his time with you and your brother like he used to do."

"Debra, I'm not that busy. Tonya and JJ are always welcome." He hugged Tonya. "Your mom, dad and I will discuss it and come up with a date."

Tonya threw her arms around his neck. "*Yay!* I love you, Uncle."

"Love you, too, kiddo." In that instant, he felt the pull of fatherhood and his heart nearly burst. He had no idea how Londyn felt about the subject, and he worried about her being in the high-risk category. Braxton brought his wayward musings to a screeching halt. He was getting way ahead of himself. He hadn't even told the woman he loved her and here he sat thinking about babies and parenthood.

"Okay, everybody," his mother called. "Dinner's ready."

Everyone filed into the dining room and took their usual places around the large table with seating for ten. His father said a blessing, then they filled their plates and dug in. More than once, Braxton caught his mother staring at him, then the empty chair next to him. He shrugged and continued to eat. Luckily, the conversation turned to his niece and nephew and their progress in school. They had just returned after spring break and had several projects they would be completing. Then the two talked about their extracurricular activities—basketball and track for JJ and track and dance for Tonya.

"I'm so proud of you, two. I sure hope I get to have at least another grandchild before the Lord calls me home," his mother added casually.

Every eye at the table turned Braxton's way. His mother beamed, while his father just chuckled and shook his head. Debra and Jared smothered grins and his nephew and niece outright laughed.

"Uncle B, you might want to get started," JJ said. "Forty is kind of old to be having kids."

"Forty is not *old* and how about y'all just eat and stay out of my business."

Debra burst out laughing. She held up a hand. "I'm sorry, baby bro, I can't help it."

He shot his nephew a glare and mouthed, "Just for that, I'm beating you before you get off the starting line when I come over."

JJ grinned and kept eating.

Braxton made it through the remainder of the meal without any other comments about his love life. After his sister's family left, he stayed around a while longer and ended up in the family room alone with his father.

"I hope you aren't letting your mother get to you, son. You're the only one who can decide what's right for you and Londyn."

"I'm not. I love her and I want to marry her."

Not much rendered Johnathan Harper silent, but apparently, Braxton's pronouncement did. "I didn't know things were that serious between you two."

"I know you're thinking it happened kind of fast, but—"

"But that's how the heart works sometime. There's no timetable on love, Braxton. I admit I'm a little surprised because you've never really seemed to be interested in long-term relationships, but I couldn't be happier for you. Have you talked to Londyn yet?"

"No. I haven't even told her how I feel. And it wasn't that I haven't been interested, it's just that I could never find the right one." It came to him that he should've told Londyn first, but he wanted and valued his father's advice. "Since you and Mom have made this work for forty-seven years, what do I do?" He scrubbed a hand down his face. "I mean, I'm *forty* and this is the first time I can honestly say that I've been in love."

His father laughed softly. "Again, there's no timetable. Wouldn't you rather be forty and get it right the first time than have gotten married early and got it wrong? As for what to do, love her, cherish her and respect who she is as an equal partner in your relationship. Be honest and transparent about everything, even if it's uncomfortable."

Braxton pondered his father's counsel. He'd never led Braxton down a wrong path—if anything, his steadfast love and guidance had kept Braxton on track. "Thanks, Dad." He knew what he wanted. He wanted Londyn in his life forever.

# CHAPTER 10

*T*hursday evening, Londyn sat at her desk entering chart notes on the new computer system.

"How late are you planning to work?"

Londyn glanced over at the wall clock that read five-fifteen. "Seven, seven-thirty. Are you leaving?"

Shawn shoved his hands in his pockets. "In about ten minutes." He nodded toward the computer. "I see you're enjoying the network."

She smiled. "I knew we were in the technology dark ages, but I didn't realize how far back until now. I feel like a kid on Christmas morning." Not only could she pull up her charts with ease, but she could also input her schedule so Corinne could see it without Londyn having to print it out, or leave notes about any changes.

He laughed. "I know what you mean. I thought Corinne was going to kiss Gayle when she finished the installation. You know she baked the woman chocolate chip cookies."

"Are you kidding?" She leaned back in her chair. "I saw her out there yesterday doing a little dance at her desk. I guess she's happy."

"We all are. Speaking of computers, are you still seeing that guy."

She'd known he would bring the subject up sooner or later. "Yes, I'm still seeing *Braxton*. Why?"

"Just curious. I hadn't seen him around and thought maybe things had cooled between you two."

"You're persistent, if nothing else." Londyn rolled her eyes and opened the next chart. "I'll see you tomorrow."

"Goodnight."

After he left, she worked steadily over the next hour. She'd been putting in one or two extra hours each night that week to get her charts digitized. Most of the other psychologists had decided to take their time, but Londyn wanted to get up and running sooner, rather than later. Her cell chimed and she smiled.

Braxton: *Hey, baby. What are you doing later tonight?*

Londyn: *Working for another hour or so. What did you have in mind?*

Braxton: *I could stop by your place in a couple of hours and bring dinner. Just let me know what you want.*

She typed back that she wanted something light like a shrimp Caesar salad. Her thumb hovered over the Send button as a wicked thought came to her. Smiling, she deleted the message, did a Google search, found the image she wanted and downloaded it. She opened the text message box: *This is what I want.* She attached the photo of Prince's symbol with the words "Do Me, Baby" on it and hit Send.

Londyn giggled and resumed typing. Ten minutes later, her phone rang. "Hey, handsome."

"Come open the door, baby," Braxton said.

She sat up straight. "You're here?" Even as she asked, she grabbed her keys and hurried out front to let him in.

"Where else would I be after you sent me a message like that?"

She locked the door behind him. Something in his expression gave her pause. He hadn't cracked a smile and his breathing was labored.

"Are you here alone?"

"Yes."

"Good." He swept her in his arms, strode down the hall to her office and kicked the door closed. He placed her on her feet. Reaching around her, he turned the lock.

Londyn, with her back against the door, looked up at him. "What are you doing?"

His hand skimmed up her bare thigh beneath her dress. "Giving you exactly what you asked for."

A feral grin curved his lips when he knew she realized what he had in mind. He didn't give her a chance to reply. His mouth came down on hers...*hard*. His tongue swirled around hers in a kiss so devastatingly erotic it left her gasping for breath and pulsing everywhere. She nearly came right then. She moaned at the feeling of his hard body pressed against hers. Londyn ran her hands up his strong arms and over his muscular chest.

Braxton dropped to his knees, still holding her dress and slid his tongue from her inner thigh to her core, then dragged her panties down and off. "I broke every speed limit to get to you," he said, his voice hoarse with need.

Any coherent thought she might have had left her mind and she couldn't answer him if her life depended on it. Londyn cried out when his mouth clamped down on her core. The hot stroke of his tongue over her clit sent jolts of pleasure coursing through her body and she trembled. He stroked her deeper and feasted like a man indulging in his favorite treat. She moaned and gripped his head to keep him in place as her hips rocked against his mouth. "Braxton," she said, gasping for breath. Her thighs involuntarily locked around his head, but he held them apart, bringing her to a blinding orgasm that had her shaking uncontrollably and screaming his name.

Braxton rose to his feet, dropped his pants and rolled a condom over his thick erection. He grasped her buttocks and lifted her in his arms. Bracing her against the door, he entered her with one long thrust.

She closed her eyes as she reveled in the sensation of him inside her. He didn't move for several seconds and she opened her eyes.

He leaned his forehead against hers. "I love you, Londyn."

Her heart pounded faster and harder. "What did you say?" she whispered, not believing she'd heard him correctly.

"I said I love you."

"I love you, too." As if that was what he'd been waiting for, he began moving, plunging deep and retreating in a slow, erotic cadence that sent heat spiraling through her. She moaned. His thrusts came faster and faster and their passionate cries bounced off the walls. Londyn gripped his shoulders. Each well-placed thrust went deeper and deeper, and touched a part of her that no man had ever reached. Then she was crying and coming in a dizzying explosion of pleasure.

Braxton withdrew and carried her over to her desk. He placed her on her feet and turned her around, then unzipped her dress and removed it, leaving her clad in just her purple lace bra. "Now, I'm going to do you from behind."

She braced her hands on the desk as he surged back inside. Londyn screamed his name again. He leaned down and rained kisses along her spine.

I'm going to work your body in every way and give you everything you want," he said in a heated rush.

His words and the scorching heat of his tongue sent pinpoints of pleasure down her nerve endings. "Don't stop."

"I won't stop until you ask me to, until I do you in every way you want. Until you can't handle any more."

Londyn gasped. He whispered a mixture of tender endearments and erotic promises that made her desire climb even higher. Their breathing grew louder as he gripped her tighter and drove into her harder. The pressure built inside her with an intensity she'd never felt, and she convulsed and screamed his name as waves of ecstasy crashed through her so violently she thought she might pass out.

Braxton thrust, once, twice, then stiffened and exploded inside her with a harsh groan of male satisfaction. He collapsed on top of her, one hand on the desk, so as not to put all of his weight on her.

Straightening, he turned her to face him and kissed her tenderly. Her heart felt so full she thought it would burst.

"More?"

Chuckling tiredly, she said, "I don't think I can handle any more." *I can't believe I just had sex in my office.* But she felt no remorse. Just pure satisfaction.

He smiled. "Don't you want me to touch you, kiss you, give you pleasure, make you come, then do you all over again?" he murmured while caressing her breasts and skating his tongue along her neck.

A shudder raced through her. "Yes. Follow me home."

"All you ever have to do is ask."

Londyn cleaned up her desk and walked to the back of the building. She pressed several buttons on a panel near the rear door and activated the silent alarm before locking the door.

Braxton escorted her to her car. "I'll be right behind you."

She tossed him a bold wink. "I'm counting on it." She wanted him to *do her* for the rest of her life.

"Well look who's here," Dani said when Braxton walked into the Double Trouble Friday evening. "You're all dressed up and looking good. Hot date?"

"Something like that."

"I guess you took my advice about relaxing your exacting standards."

Braxton smiled. "Actually, I didn't. Londyn isn't perfect, but she's as close to it as a person can get. Even more, she's the perfect woman for me."

She wrapped her arms around him. "Aw, give me a hug. I'm so happy for you, for all three of you."

"Thanks, Dani." He walked to the other side of the bar where Cole and Axel sat. He'd asked them to meet him for a few minutes. "What's up?" They did a fist bump.

"That's what I want to know," Axel said. He glanced down at his watch.

"I know you and Naphressa have plans, so this won't take long."

"We're going to have to find another night to hook up, since Fridays seem to be out these days," Cole said.

"Probably. Anyway, I wanted you to know that I'm going to propose to Londyn."

Wide grins filled his friends faces and Cole said, "Congrats, man. That was quick."

He laughed and spread his hands. "Hey, I can't help it if she finds me irresistible."

Axel slapped him on the back. "Congratulations. When do you plan to do it?"

"Hopefully, tonight." Braxton would be picking her up in half an hour for their dinner date. Unconsciously, he touched his pocket where he'd placed the small velvet box.

"We need to toast." Cole signaled a bartender. Once they each had drinks, he lifted his glass. "Here's to becoming an irresistible husband."

They touched glasses and tossed back the amber liquid. "I'll see you later. Oh, and, Cole, don't say anything to Dani."

Cole laughed. "I won't. Let us know how it turns out."

"I will." Smiling, Braxton threw up a wave to Dani on his way out."

His smile was still in place when he arrived to pick up Londyn. She opened the door wearing another dress that hugged her curves. "You're killing me with these dresses."

"It's only fair because you've been killing me since I saw you on that dance floor moving this sexy body." Londyn slid her arms up his chest and wound them around his neck.

He groaned when she pressed her body close against his. "Baby, I need you to stop tempting me. We have reservations and I intend to keep them." He gently removed her arms and took a step back.

She laughed softly. "Still having problems with that spontaneity thing, huh?"

Braxton lifted a brow. "You're saying that after what happened last night?" He had never done anything as impulsive as he'd done last night. When she'd sent that text, it had been all he could do to keep his sanity long enough to get to her office. He'd been in such a hurry he was halfway down the block before he remembered the condoms. He hadn't lied about breaking speed limits and was lucky that the cops hadn't spotted him. As far as spontaneity went, Braxton had never, *ever* had sex in an office.

"Okay, okay, I'll let you off the hook for now."

He smiled. "You can tempt me later."

"You've got a deal, love."

Every time she used an endearment made his heart shout for joy. Braxton knew he was probably grinning like an idiot, but he didn't care. Once in his car, he got them underway and ended at another expensive steakhouse.

They continued laughing and talking after being seated and their orders taken. It was as if their declarations of love had freed them. It had certainly freed him in ways he had yet to understand. Her eyes met his and revealed passion and something he'd never seen before—love. Braxton had a hard time concentrating on his meal because the hunger he felt had nothing to do with food and everything to do with the beautiful woman sitting across from him.

"My parents want to meet you," Londyn said, halfway through dinner.

"Okay." He figured it was probably time for him to meet them anyway.

She eyed him. "You're okay with that?"

He shrugged. "Yes, why wouldn't I be? Besides, you've met mine already, so it's only fair." He chuckled at the confused look on her face. Reaching for her hand, he said, "Londyn, I love you, and I'm in this for the long haul. It's time your parents knew this, too. See what their schedule is like for next weekend. Maybe we can all go out to breakfast. My treat."

She squeezed his hand. "My mom is going to lose her mind over you."

Laughter poured out of him. "I hope so."

Shaking her head, Londyn went back to her dinner.

When they finished, Braxton took a deep breath and grasped her hand again. "Londyn, I—" Londyn gasped, her eyes widening as if she'd seen a ghost. Her hand trembled in his and she bore an expression he'd never seen. Frowning, he glimpsed over his shoulder and saw a man of average height approaching.

"Well, if it isn't my long-lost fiancée."

*Fiancée?* Braxton whipped his head around and stared at Londyn.

She shot the man an angry glare. "I'm not your *anything!*" she snapped. "Get away from me."

The man took a step closer and Braxton came to his feet, towering over him by a good five or six inches. "You heard the lady. Leave!"

He looked Braxton up and down and an evil grin curved his

lips. "Did she tell you about her little problem in the bedroom? That she can't please a man?"

Londyn looked stricken.

"Don't say another word to her," Braxton whispered harshly. "You have one second to leave this table, or I'm going to *kick your ass!*"

"Yeah, right."

The words were barely out of the man's mouth when Braxton snatched him by the throat and said with lethal calmness, "Maybe I didn't make myself clear. You are leaving this restaurant now. Walking or carried out, your choice. My temper's not real good right now, so I don't think you want to test me." Braxton tossed him aside—none—too gently and the man stumbled backward, crashing into a diner at a nearby table. Every person in the room was focused on them, and he saw a manager rushing toward the table. Braxton apologized for the disruption and took his seat. He could count on one hand the number of times he'd lost his temper and each of the instances had to do with someone threatening someone he loved. He dragged a hand down his face. "I'm sorry for embarrassing you, Londyn." That was his only regret.

Londyn, stared at him, her expression the same. "I…I…"

He caressed her hand. "Sweetheart, are you okay? He's gone." He had about a million questions running through his head, but Londyn was his only concern at the moment.

"Take me home, Braxton," she said with tears filling her eyes, her voice barely audible. "*Please.*"

"Of course, baby." He led her to the front, caught the attention of their server and gestured for the bill. The young woman seemed to understand their plight and quickly brought it over. Braxton paid it, leaving a generous tip, then escorted Londyn to the car. She sat almost curled up and so close to the door that if it opened she'd fall out, and didn't say a word. She wouldn't even look at him. He could feel her withdrawing from him minute by minute and it broke his heart. By the time they made it to her house, she still hadn't said anything.

Londyn dropped down on one corner of her sofa without removing her coat and curled up in a ball.

Braxton squatted in front of her and stroked her cheek. "What do you need me to do for you, Londyn? Tell me how I can help you."

"Please leave."

Icy tentacles of fear slid down his spine. "I can't do that. I'm not leaving you like this. I don't know why he said those things to you, but their lies, honey."

Without warning, she jumped up, almost knocking him over. "You have no idea what he did to me," she shouted.

"No, I don't," he said, rising from the floor and trying to keep his voice soft and calm. "But if you tell me, maybe we can fix it together." He reached for her and she slapped his hands away. *She* was the trained clinician, not him, but his baby was hurting and he had to do something.

Londyn rounded on him, her hazel eyes blazing in anger. "You can't fix this. You can't fix *me*." She hit her palm against her chest.

"Londyn—"

"He wanted me to act like those women in the porn movies. Men always do."

Braxton felt his eyes widen and his chest tighten. "Not all men are like that, sweetheart."

"Are you going to stand there and tell me you've *never* watched pornography?"

"No," he said slowly. "But—"

"I knew it. You'll change just like the rest of them." She marched over and snatched the door open. "Get out."

Stunned, he couldn't move. "Londyn, wait a minute." He didn't need a psychology degree to know she was having some sort of PTSD episode and he wondered if she had ever gone to counseling herself. "We don't have to talk about this anymore tonight."

"We aren't going to talk about it ever." Her face went blank. She had effectively shut him out.

Not knowing what else to do and afraid his staying would make it worse, he did as she asked. As soon as she closed the door, he heard her gut-wrenching sobs. He lifted his hand to knock, but instead placed his palm against it, the pieces of his heart shattering, and he had no idea what to do. Braxton's steps were heavy as he walked into the waiting elevator car and rode down to the bottom floor.

When the doors opened, he started for the exit. Halfway through the lobby he froze. Everything came back to him in a rush. *You can strip for me next time,* he'd said that first time they'd made love, and she'd hesitated briefly. *I'm working on it,* she'd told him during their conversation during lunch at the deli when he asked if she'd been able to help her client. *She* was the woman, the reason she'd specialized in treating people with sex and pornography addictions. It all made sense now—the moments of vulnerability, the sadness.

Braxton spun around and took determined strides back to the elevator. He wasn't leaving her. Not now. Not ever.

# CHAPTER 11

*A*s soon as the door closed, Londyn collapsed on the floor next to it and sobbed. *I thought it was over. I thought I was okay.* Seeing Antoine and hearing him spew those ugly words had ripped the scab off the wound she had desperately been trying to heal. She thought she had, but now Braxton would never see her the same again. And that he'd confessed to watching pornography had made it worse. What if he became like Antoine—demanding that they view the movies before sex and re-enacting the scenes, no matter how demeaning they were for her? She couldn't put herself through that again. Londyn wanted to believe that Braxton wouldn't change, that he loved her, but her mind was so jumbled.

She brought her knees up to her chest and dropped her head, the tears she had held back for two years coming in waves like a broken dam. She didn't know how long she had been on the floor when the pounding on her door startled her.

"Londyn, open the door, baby. I'm not leaving you."

"Go away, Braxton."

"No. And unless you want your neighbors, the police and

everybody else who's going to show up because of all this noise to know what's going on, I suggest you unlock the door."

Londyn knew he was right. It wouldn't take much for the people in the building to call the police. Management frowned on any type of disturbance. Reluctantly, she reached up and unlocked the door, but made no attempt to get up.

Braxton came in, closed the door behind him and joined her on the floor. "I love you Londyn, and I'm not walking away from us. I've waited too long to find you to just give up." He grasped her hand and kissed the back. "You asked me if I've ever watched pornography and I answered truthfully. But that was more than a decade and a half ago and I haven't even thought about it since then. When you described the addiction to me, I admit that it made me think about some things." He paused briefly, as if getting his thoughts together. "I remember never finding fulfilment in my sexual encounters and I wondered if I had subconsciously been looking for that same kind of excitement. I realize now that it was never the women, it was me."

Londyn went still. He must have felt it because he gave her hand a gentle squeeze and placed a soft kiss on her temple.

He shifted to face her. "I wasn't addicted by any part of the definition and I have *never* asked a woman to do any of those things you described. I don't plan to start. You have given me more pleasure than I thought possible and I don't need any other outside stimulation. Just you. I can't undo all the things he did to you, but I can love you. If you want us to go talk to someone, I'm down. If you want it to be just you, I'm down for that, too. I promise to take you there and wait, so you'll know that you're not alone. That you're loved, cherished and supported. I'll do all of it for you."

A tear slid down her cheek. This man had just bared his soul to her and promised to be there for whatever she needed, including counseling and he wasn't even the cause of her problems. She could do no less. Gathering herself, Londyn haltingly and painstakingly shared how her relationship changed with Antoine after they became engaged, from his initial insistence that they watch pornography together to demanding she "perform" like the actresses on the screen. "I suggested he go to counseling, but he told me he didn't have a problem and promised it wouldn't happen again, that he'd stop watching porn. But he didn't." She found out he'd been missing work, and every time they were together after that point, he had his phone out searching online for porn sites. His false vow had barely lasted a week. "He asked me to stop by his place because he said he had a special surprise for me and..." Her voice faltered.

Braxton lifted her onto his lap and wrapped his arms around her. "It's okay, baby. I will never let him hurt you again."

Drawing strength from Braxton's protective embrace, she continued, "As soon as he opened the door, he grabbed me and said he wanted us to have rough sex. I told him no, told him we were done, and started to leave, but he wouldn't let me. He ripped my blouse and tried to force himself on me, saying if I'd loosen up, then he wouldn't have to watch porn, but I kept fighting." Her stomach started churning just as it did on that day. "Then...then a woman I had never seen came from his bedroom, naked, and said to let me go, that a threesome is only good when everybody's into it. That's when I threw his ring at him and ran out." Braxton's arms tightened around her. "Ow, you're squeezing me."

"I'm sorry. Why didn't you report it to the police?"

Though it all occurred over the span of a month, because of the emotional impact, it felt much longer. "Because I shouldn't have let it happen. I felt degraded and embarrassed. Here I was a clinical psychologist, allowing to happen to me the very things I tell my patients they should escape. He made me feel like trash."

Braxton lifted her until she straddled his lap and cradled her face between his large hands. "Listen to me, Londyn. None of what he did is your fault. *He's* the one with the problem."

"I thought you would think less of me. I'm sorry for believing you would be just like him. I'm sorry for saying those things to you. You're nothing like him." Clinically, she did understand why she'd lashed out at him. Seeing Antoine had triggered an emotional crisis. The façade of pretending that everything was okay, when in reality, she was still very much broken inside, had finally taken its toll.

"No apologies needed, but I have to tell you if I ever see him again, it's going to be hard for me to keep from hurting him the same way he hurt you." Anger radiated from him. He closed his eyes briefly. "You are my heart, and I won't ever allow *anyone* to hurt or disrespect you again."

His words broke the last barrier around her and the tears started again.

"You've tried to deal with this on your own for so long. You don't have to anymore. I'm here. I'll always be here."

She nodded and buried her face in his neck, too mentally drained to process his words. Gradually, her tears stopped and only her periodic shuddering breaths ruffled the silence.

Braxton eased them off the floor and carried her to her bedroom where he stripped them both, pulled back the covers on her bed and placed her in the center. He laid down next to her and gathered her in his embrace. "Rest, baby."

The rhythmic sound of his strong heart beating beneath her ear relaxed her and her breathing slowed. She loved this man with everything in her.

Braxton had delayed meeting Londyn's parents for two weeks because after everything she'd told him, he felt they needed time to just work on being together. He'd been so worried that he had her pack her bags, then brought her to his home so he could keep an eye on her. They hadn't made love, but lying next to her each night he felt the same contentment as if they had. He'd also gotten used to waking up next to her and sharing breakfast. Londyn had decided against seeing a counselor for the time being, citing that Braxton had helped her purge the demons that plagued her, but she did promise to seek help in the future, if necessary. Although, he had some reservations, he deferred to her because she was the expert.

"I'm ready."

He turned from where he stood in his kitchen staring out at the backyard and smiled. She had on a pair of black crop pants, a short-sleeved top and black flats. After their Saturday morning breakfast with her parents, they were going to take advantage of the warm spring weather and have a picnic at Piedmont Park. "So am I. I still wish your parents would've let me take you all out." Her mother had vehemently refused to allow him to pay and, instead, said she would prepare the meal at home.

Londyn smiled. "I could've told you my mom was going to overrule you."

Seeing her relaxed and happy made his heart swell. "But you didn't, so you owe me brownies."

She hooked her arm in his. "Come on and quit complaining. I told you, you'll get your brownies."

Braxton bent and slanted his mouth over hers in a deep, sensual kiss. "I'm going to hold you to it."

"I know."

Following her directions, he parked in the driveway of a Brookhaven home on a tree-lined street with stately homes and meticulously maintained lawns. The front porch held two rocking chairs with a small table between them. Before they got out of the car, the front door opened and a tall, elegant woman stepped out with features so reminiscent of Londyn's, he knew what Londyn would look like in twenty years. He held Londyn's hand as they headed across the cobblestone walkway and up the three steps to the porch.

"Hi, Mom." Londyn embraced her mother. She turned to Braxton. "Braxton, I'd like you to meet my mother, Paulette Grant. Mom, this is Braxton Harper."

"It's a pleasure to meet you, Mrs. Grant. You have a beautiful home."

"Thank you, Braxton. It's a pleasure to meet you, too. You all come inside. Breakfast is ready."

An older man about the same height as Braxton, whose expression conveyed authority and challenge—meant to intimidate—stood in the middle of the living room. It was the same look Braxton's father had worn when Jared met the family for the first time. Strangely, it didn't bother Braxton one bit. He would face down her father as many times as necessary for Londyn.

Londyn flew into her father's outstretched arms. "Dad, I want you to meet Braxton Harper. Braxton, my father, Dwight Grant."

Looking him directly in the eyes, Braxton firmly shook the older man's hand. "Pleasure to meet you, sir."

Mr. Grant's eyebrows shot up. "It's good to meet you, too, Braxton. Londyn, why don't you help your mother bring everything to the table, so Braxton and I can chat."

*More like interrogate,* Braxton thought with a smile. Londyn clearly didn't want to leave, but her mother took hold of Londyn's arm and steered her out of the room.

"Have a seat, Braxton," he said, gesturing to one of two chairs flanking a sofa.

He sat and waited for Mr. Grant to take the other one.

"Londyn tells me you work with computers."

"I design computer networks for small and large companies." He shared his educational background and told how long he'd been in the field. The rapid-fire questions continued, ranging from information about his family to hobbies. Braxton answered them all without missing a beat.

Mr. Grant leaned forward in his chair and clasped his hands together. "What are your intentions toward my daughter?"

He didn't hesitate. "I love Londyn and I plan to ask her to marry me...with your permission, of course."

A smile broke out on the man's face and he chuckled. "You say with my permission, but your expression clearly says you're going to ask her whether I like it or not."

"No disrespect intended, sir, but yes, I am. I will love her, protect her, cherish her and above all respect her as long as I draw breath."

Mr. Grant stood and extended his hand. "None taken, and you have my blessing. I've waited a long time for my baby girl to find someone like you. I don't have to worry about her now."

Braxton followed suit, clasping the man's hand and grinned. "You won't ever have to worry about her."

He nodded and clapped Braxton on the shoulder. "Welcome to the family, son."

"Thanks."

Breakfast was a leisurely affair that reminded Braxton of his own family gatherings. Mrs. Grant and his mother were so similar, he instinctively knew the two women would get along well. She had blushed with his compliments, while Londyn rolled her eyes. They lingered at the table for another hour laughing and talking before saying their goodbyes.

"Braxton, it was so nice to finally meet you. You'll have to come back for dinner soon," Mrs. Grant said, her arm hooked in his as they walked out to his car.

"Does that invitation include me, too, Mom?" Londyn asked. "You were so interested in Braxton, you barely remembered I was here."

"Oh, baby, of course you're included."

Hugs and promises to return were made, then Braxton and Londyn headed to Piedmont Park.

"I told you my mom was going to be all over you," Londyn grumbled. "Giggling like you were her date, instead of mine. '*Oh, Braxton, this old outfit,*'" she mimicked in falsetto. The comment had been in response to Braxton telling her how nice she looked.

"Aw, baby, don't hate."

She rolled her eyes, but couldn't hide her smile. "I'm thinking I should get something for feeling like an outcast with my own parents."

He slanted her a quick glance. "I'll get you anything you want."

"*Anything?* I'm going to think real hard about it, too, because it has to be something better than good."

Braxton threw his head back and roared with laughter. He turned up the music and hummed along, knowing he already had something better than good in store. He parked and went around to the passenger side of the car to help Londyn out.

"I thought you said we were having a picnic," Londyn said, eying him curiously.

He flashed her a grin. "We are."

"I didn't see any food." She peered into the backseat.

Smiling, he ran a finger down her nose. "That's because I did everything while you were asleep." He opened the trunk by remote and removed a soft-side cooler and roll-up picnic blanket with an attached carrying strap. "How about we go for a walk first?" he asked, closing the trunk.

"That's fine. I'll take the blanket."

Once inside the park, they opted for one of the walking trails. Reaching for her free hand, he entwined their fingers and they started on a leisurely stroll. As they walked, neither of them attempted to initiate conversation. He assumed, just like him, she preferred to savor the warm spring afternoon. A gentle breeze blew across Braxton's face and he experienced a peace and contentment he'd never known. After a while, they retraced their steps and sought out a spot for their picnic and decided to spread their blanket under the shade of a large oak tree.

Londyn glanced around the park. "Mmm, this is nice, peaceful. What's for lunch?"

Braxton unearthed bowls filled with fixings for her favorite shrimp Caesar salad, fruit, French baguette slices, and sparkling lemonade. "I didn't know what your mom intended to prepare for breakfast, so I fixed something light. It's a good thing, too." Her mother had made thick Belgian waffles with warm homemade maple syrup, fluffy scrambled eggs, bacon, sausage, fruit, and yogurt.

"Yeah, she kind of went overboard. I should've packed up a few of those waffles to take home." She popped a grape in her mouth.

"Since homemade bread isn't my forte, we'll have to make do with the store-bought kind."

Laughing, Londyn laid a hand on his arm. "If you're going to take the time to do all this, I'll eat whatever you make." She sobered. "Thank you for loving me, for helping me to heal. When I'm with you, I feel safe and I know everything is going to be okay."

Her words and the tears shimmering in her eyes melted his heart. Emotion clogged his throat, and he fought for control. All he needed was to lose his man card by bawling like a baby in the middle of a park. "My love," he whispered, just before placing a sweet kiss on her lips. Braxton wiped away the lingering moisture on her cheeks with the pad of his thumb. "You can fix yours first." While she assembled her salad, he poured them glasses of lemonade and placed them on coasters. He made his own plate and they ate while talking about everything and nothing.

She set aside her empty plate. "That was so good and just

enough. I'm curious about dessert, though. You can't have a good picnic without it," she teased.

He chuckled. "I've got you covered." He reached inside the cooler and handed her a cellophane bag tied with purple ribbon.

Her eyes lit up. "Ooh, an edible chocolate box." She shook it. "With goodies inside. And a purple ribbon."

Braxton smiled inwardly. She was right about there being *goodies* inside. He watched as she opened it, his heart beating a mile a minute.

Londyn carefully lifted the lid. "I love chocolate, and I'm going to eat every one of these pieces in—. Oh. My. *Goodness.*" Her gaze flew to his. "Is this what I think it is?"

"I don't know. You'll have to open it to find out."

Her hands shook as she retrieved the small blue velvet box. "Braxton."

He eased the box from her hands and moved closer to her. He opened it and the diamond solitaire surrounded by alternating diamond and amethyst baguettes sparkled in the sunlight. He had chosen the purple gem because of her love for Prince. It also happened to be her birthstone. "Londyn, you captured my heart from the moment I met you. I want to spend the rest of my life laughing with you, crying with you, protecting you and loving you. Oh, and *doing* you."

She laughed through her tears.

"I promise to do everything in my power to make you happy. Will you marry me?"

"Yes, *yes!*"

He slid the ring on her finger and she launched herself at him.

"This has been the best day of my life. I love you, Braxton."

"I love you, too, baby. Forever." He'd finally found his perfect woman.

# EPILOGUE

*S*ix weeks later.

It seemed like forever before Braxton heard the words he'd been waiting for since he proposed to Londyn. She hadn't wanted a long engagement and he was more than happy to accommodate her. Of course, they had nearly given their mothers heart failure. Faced with the ultimatum of having his baby's June wedding or elopement, the two women had quickly pulled themselves together and had coordinated a wedding fit for a queen. His queen.

"You may now kiss the bride."

The words had barely left the minister's tongue before Braxton captured Londyn's mouth in a hungry kiss that stunned him in its intensity. All the love he felt for her rose up so strongly, it almost overwhelmed him. He registered the sound of throats clearing, but he kept right on kissing his wife. *My wife.* At length, he lifted his head. "You are my everything."

Londyn smiled up at him and touched his face. "And you are mine."

Still smiling, he glanced over his shoulder at his two best men and mouthed, "Thank you." Cole and Axel's friendship meant everything to him. After the minister's pronouncement, he had to endure an hour of pictures when all he wanted was to take Londyn somewhere, *anywhere*, strip her naked and show her just how much he liked her dress. He had been in a constant state of arousal since the moment she walked down the aisle to him. She looked stunning in the white satin off-the-shoulder sleeveless gown adorned with pearls and rhinestones that hugged the curves he loved so much. It dipped in the front to give him a hint of cleavage and left her back completely bare. And each time Londyn turned and he got a glimpse of it, pushed him closer to his limit. When they finally settled into the limousine that would take them to the hotel where their reception was being held, he was two seconds away from snapping.

"Are you okay?" Londyn searched his face with concern.

"I will be as soon as I can get you alone and naked."

She laughed. "We're of the same mind." Hiking up her dress, she straddled him on the seat and ground her body against his.

"What are you doing?" he gritted out as a shudder passed through him.

"I'm going to do you in ways you can't imagine, from today until eternity," she murmured sensually, trailing kisses along his jaw.

His breath came in short gasps. "We can't do that here."

"Oh, but we can, my love." She pressed a button and the privacy window rose.

"Does this fall under the category of being spontaneous?" Braxton had done more impulsive things in the last four months since meeting Londyn than he had in his entire life. He had to admit that kind of liked it. Especially at this moment.

She angled her head thoughtfully and smiled. "I hadn't thought about it that way, but, yes, we can file it under spontaneity. Also, it's going to take at least forty-five minutes to get to the hotel. I chose that one specifically for this reason. Any more questions?" she asked with a raised brow.

He felt the slide of his zipper, then her hand slip inside his underwear and close around his erection. His breath hissed out. "Not one." Braxton lifted his body to facilitate the removal of his pants and boxer briefs.

"Good. Now get me out of this dress."

Braxton carefully removed her dress and laid it over the other seat with his pants, leaving her clad in those rhinestone heels she'd worn on their first date and a purple jeweled thong. He cursed under his breath and grew even harder.

Londyn straddled him once again. "Besides, with you being forty and all, I figured we should probably get started on making babies."

He went still. Things had happened so fast that they hadn't really talked about having children. "You want children?"

"I do."

"So do I, baby."

"Braxton?"

"Yes, sweetheart," he said, holding her gaze.

"I don't hate weddings anymore. I love them, and I love you." She lifted one long, toned leg, straddled his body and lowered herself slowly onto his erection, swirling her hips in a figure eight.

Braxton sucked in a sharp breath. "I love you, too." And he looked forward to being with her this way for the rest of their lives.

# Don't miss the other books in this enticing & sexy series!

*Just when he thought finding a wife was out of his reach...*

Colton "Cole" Eubanks is laser focused on building wealth and settling down with a special woman before he turns forty. Accomplishing one out of two isn't bad. Unfortunately, there's no 'love of his life' on the horizon, unless he counts the one woman who's been starring in his nightly dreams—Malaya Radcliff.

After being dependent on one person after another for years, Malaya has finally learned to stand on her own. There's only one thing she hasn't been able to accomplish—gain full custody of her daughter. Her ex-husband never fights fair. His wealth always wins. This time Malaya's determined to come out on top.

So when Cole, the man she's been secretly in lust with for over a year, makes her an offer she'd be crazy to refuse, Malaya wants to say yes. But that means sacrificing her newfound independence. Yet, his enticing proposal has her thinking—why not?

Hard-working corporate attorney Axel Becker has tried settling down in the past, but when the relationship didn't work out, he focused on his career to the exclusion of everything else. Enter, Naphressa St. James. The sexy project manager is a former lover and reminds him of what his life could be—fun, exciting. She's just the woman he might need to shake him out of a rut, but convincing her they belong together will be a lot harder than he expected.

Naphressa admits she and Axel have chemistry, but she's not looking for marriage—again. Been there, done that. Except the more time she spends with Axel, the more she finds the idea of settling down with him to be downright...irresistible.

# ABOUT THE AUTHOR

Sheryl Lister is a multi-award-winning author and has enjoyed reading and writing for as long as she can remember. She is a former pediatric occupational therapist with over twenty years of experience, and resides in California. Sheryl is a wife, mother of three daughters and a son-in-love, and grandmother to two special little boys. When she's not writing, Sheryl can be found on a date with her husband or in the kitchen creating appetizers. For more information, visit her website at www.sheryllister.com.

instagram.com/sheryllister

Her Passionate Promise

Love's Sweet Kiss (Sassy Seasoned Sisters #1)

Never Letting Go (Carnivale Chronicles)

Embracing Ever After (Once Upon a Baby #1)